About the Author

Isabella Renee was raised in California and moved to New York City in her early twenties. She is currently enrolled in college earning a degree in History, a subject that she absolutely loves. She lives a quiet life with her cat, Bedelia, and her tortoise, Walter. Isabella has always been interested in writing, her first publication dating back to the second grade.

He & I

Isabella Renee

He & I

Olympia Publishers
London

www.olympiapublishers.com
OLYMPIA PAPERBACK EDITION

A CIP catalogue record for this title is
available from the British Library.

ISBN: 978-1-80074-744-9

This is a work of fiction.
Names, characters, places and incidents originate from the writer's
imagination. Any resemblance to actual persons, living or dead, is
purely coincidental.

First Published in 2022

Olympia Publishers
Tallis House
2 Tallis Street
London
EC4Y 0AB

Printed in Great Britain

Dedication

For Skylar, who *always* believed I could, especially when I
didn't

Acknowledgements

Thank you. To Grammy Severe, who has always supported me, I love you so much. To my mom, who has loved me, even when I'm loud and obnoxious. To my friends, Abigail and Savanna, for simply being there, and to my dad, for being an asshole.

Chapter 1

If you meet my mother, please don't tell her we met on the internet.

My fingertips must have been just as anxious as I was, they seemed to type it faster than I could think of it. When I look back on my life, I can still vividly feel the apprehension I'd felt when putting myself online. Dating websites had quickly turned into the biggest cliché of the century, it's where all the underaged men and women came to find a good quickie. I didn't want sex, I was desperate. Not desperate enough to not find the questionnaire on the website mocking, but obviously enough to open it. I had thoroughly ridiculed myself. As if I wasn't already lacking, drowning in my own desperation for companionship just wasn't enough, I had to further my frustrations by belligerent self-deprecation. I'd convinced myself that this was okay, it was nearly the holiday season and I couldn't bear the thought of being alone again. *Could anybody?* I'd thought, which is what drove my madness. I never enjoyed the thought of being alone, not even for a second. As you could imagine, the thought of dying alone had the potential to cause a panic attack.

So, as I lie here, alone in a hospital bed, I can't help but feel abandoned. I can't help but think; where the fuck is my husband? I read somewhere that at the end of your life, right before everything begins to fade, you'll see your entire life flash before your eyes in the last seven minutes. Through my original outrage, I was able to have found the slightest bit of tranquility in myself when I closed my eyes and saw Johnny. My life never truly began until I met him. He'd hearted my profile within the day I created it and it stayed that way for nearly a week. I hadn't had the nerve to send him a message. It'd been nailed into my head at a very young age that it was inappropriate to talk to strangers and I was apprehensive about it even as an adult. I dedicated a few hours a day to sitting in front of the computer, staring at his profile and trying to find the right words to say to him. I would start to type a sentence, then delete it. Over and over until I accidentally hit send. I stared at the screen in absolute disbelief for quite some time before I started to quietly laugh at myself. The only thing I could do was hope for a response. Which was another few hours a day dedicated to staring at his chat bubbles popping up and down. It was as if he was teasing me, or maybe he didn't know what to say either. I immediately dreaded not knowing what he thought of me, did he think I was funny? Did he think I was pathetic? Did I scare him away by caring too much about what my mother thought?

Johnny had a very specific way of making me feel absolutely crazy. He nearly always waited far too long to speak or respond. It was his way of telling me that he never knew what to say when I'd prefer him to tell me exactly what he was thinking. He appeared incredibly shy and reserved, he acted as such until we'd reach privacy. Behind locked doors, he was charming and affectionate. His attentiveness was just as closeted as he was, even after all the years of love I'd given him, he'd still walk into a public room as a withdrawn straight man and he'd look at me as such. This time must have been different. When I saw him walk into my empty hospital room, it didn't seem as though he cared who was in the room. He sat at my bedside and he grabbed my face with the firmest of grips. His thumbs grazed over my cheeks to wipe dried tears and he simply kissed me. I thought I would die just then, but surely my body wouldn't betray me that way. All I wanted was to be held by him and I was. He let my face go after a few sweet seconds. I dared not say a word to him now and ruin the open affection I was receiving, though I could feel the pain he exuded. My empathy easily became overwhelming and I broke the silence.

"Johnny," I spoke to him as quietly as I could, I didn't want him to let me go. More silence followed, *now wasn't the time to not talk to me*. "Say anything," I said and it was *again* followed by silence. The sound of his breathing was almost as deafening as the absence of noise coming from his lips. I decided to let him be until he wanted to speak. I knew I wouldn't get much from him. I instead held onto his jacket to keep his body close to mine. It felt like I'd waited an eternity for him to finally speak, but when he did, it wasn't nearly as relieving as I'd wanted it to be.

"I don't want you to leave me, Frederick."

I barely heard him utter the words, he was so quiet. I felt a single tear drop onto my neck and then another. It broke my heart to hear the sadness in his voice, it broke my heart more to know I couldn't fix it this time. I took the opportunity to wrap my arms around him and hold him too. I wasn't sure if I should say anything further, I didn't know if it would only make him feel worse. We stayed this way for a while, a few minutes felt like a few seconds and he let go of me. He weaseled his way into my bed with me and intertwined his fingers through mine. I watched our hands together and imagined we were home on the sofa. It was Christmas and the lights sparkled on the tree and around the windows. We would watch; It's A Wonderful Life, and go to bed together, but this time only he would wake up because I wasn't there any more. He was alone in the holiday season just as I had been ten years ago.

"You're wearing your wedding ring." I'd noticed. I ran a single finger over the wedding band and allowed myself a moment of pure joy. Johnny *never* wore his ring, specifically so his father wouldn't find out I was more than what he wanted me to be. Seeing him wear it at all gave me just enough serotonin to be happy in this horrific situation. I watched the reflection of the bright backlit fluorescent lights in the silver of the ring, using any small thing I could find to distract myself.

I could tell he was listening to what I was saying because his breathing seemed to stop every time I spoke. As if he was surprised that I said anything to him at all. I focused again on the little distractions around me, or possibly just him. How soft his hands were, how wonderful his hair smelled. I quietly wished we could lie here forever like this. I knew he would agree with me if I was verbal with the wish, though I also knew it might jinx it if spoken aloud.

We lay there silently together for another unnoticeable amount of time before the doctor entered the room with his inevitable diagnosis. To my surprise, Johnny didn't move. He stayed put, and just as close to me as he was before someone else had entered the room. The doctor opened his mouth and spoke absolute gibberish. It felt foreign. I knew what he was saying wasn't anything reassuring, but my mind couldn't wrap around the words he spoke. He may as well have repeated 'You're not going to like what I have to say', over and over until, by force of circumstance, I started to cry. It was completely unavoidable.

'You'll abruptly leave Johnny', which is not at all what he said, but it's what I heard through the distinct Spanish he was speaking. *I wish I could speak Spanish.* Johnny always had to translate for me when we'd travel. I couldn't help but wonder if

he was going to translate for me now.

He waited until the doctor left the room again to stand up, leaving the bed. He released his grip from my hand and somehow managed to get his feet on the ground. He stood, without collapsing as I would have. I admired how much stronger he was than me, the entire world could be in flames and he would still look at me and tell me it was going to be okay. Would he do the same for me now? Or would he look at me and be honest with me? Would he explain to me the severity of the situation with a straight face, or would he break down and cry? I sat up to prepare myself for his emotions and was surprised to see his eyes well up. *Please don't cry, I can't stand it when you cry.* His palms seemed to have started to sweat. I saw him fidget with his sleeves, I assumed to distract himself. Had he forgotten how to form words? I tried to be patient with him as I knew what he'd heard was going to affect him longer than it would affect me. After some time, his silence had begun to drive me crazy, though I dared not comment on it.

I watched him open his mouth and quietly stutter to himself. It was heartbreaking to see his vulnerability make him speechless. He wasn't a man of many words but he was not often speechless. Not wanting to talk and not being able to are considerably different circumstances. There were times I'd beg him to say anything to me in a difficult situation. It would seem that this situation would be far worse than just difficult. I felt that my patience had run a bit thinner than I had expected it to and I nearly opened my mouth to speak, but then... *There it was.* The sentence that he had trouble putting together. The words I wasn't ready to accept.

"You have cancer, Frederick."

Chapter 2

A bit early to ask me to meet your mother, don't you think?

After waiting for an eternity, I had a response; I finally saw a little red one., hovering over our chatbox. I tried my best to contain my excitement. I also tried to force myself not to open it immediately. Was I supposed to wait another few days before I responded? Was that bad online dating etiquette? How could it be when he didn't say a word to me for days after I messaged him?

I took a deep breath and let it all out quicker than it went in. I stared at the message while my fingers hovered over the keyboard. What would I say back? Should I pretend to be witty? Would he be disappointed when I wasn't when we met? Would he think I lied about who I was? All questions that circled my mind as I began to type out a response to the mystery man. My responses tended to circle like a merry-go-round. I would type and then delete what I'd typed. It was an unfortunate, yet common recurrence. I'd obviously have to settle on something eventually. My stomach was actively trying to betray me. Most people would say they have butterflies in their tummy. I think it feels more like there were three small Irishmen in there doing a river dance. I thought the best course of action was to close my computer and I did so. I had thoroughly convinced myself that I shouldn't respond immediately. I told myself that if I did, he would see through to my desperation.

I lived the next two days in a constant state of irritability. I found myself checking my phone more frequently throughout the day than I normally would have. I'd only hoped my boss hadn't noticed at work. I had consequently shown up late both days as I had drifted off to sleep in front of my computer at home and slept through my alarm the next morning. I hadn't intended to become so obsessed with my new online presence. If you could even call it that. At this point it wasn't that I was trying to hide my desperation, it was that I had no idea what to say. What if he didn't like me? I stayed online for hours at a time staring at his profile picture. The entire third day seemed to drag on. Work was slow and it felt as if it had no true ending. By the time I was able to clock out and go home, I was ready for a three-century long nap. I left my phone tucked away in my desk so as not to get into trouble by constantly being on it. I took it out at the end of my shift and attempted some self-control. I slipped it into my pocket so I wouldn't sit at my desk for the next hour or more trying to think of a response. My drive home wasn't long. I lived close by. I could probably walk to work if I hadn't felt so lazy most days. When I walked into my apartment the computer immediately began to mock me. It practically begged me to open it and I, of course, gave in right away. My heart nearly beat itself out of my chest when I noticed another little red one sitting above his name. I was almost too scared to open the chatbox.

I'd love to meet her. When?

Was the contents of the next message.

It was at that point that I realized I didn't need to be anyone but myself. I read the messages over and over. He seemed so sweet, how could I not message him back? I assumed that he was joking about meeting my mother so soon. He'd never met me, why would he want to meet my mother? Unless he was being coy with me.

I want you to meet me first, I finally replied. I was completely honest. I was completely giddy. This was the first and probably only person that would message me on this website. Did I need to talk to anyone else? I looked at the computer screen again when I saw another message appear. *How thrilling.*

How's Saturday?

It was Tuesday. What a wonderful feeling of agony I'd have to endure for the next four days. Instead of telling him I didn't want to wait so long I simply complied. What else was there to say other than, I can't wait.

The details of our meeting were quickly sorted out between us. I went to bed after that and found myself unable to sleep. The little Irishmen in my stomach must have taken a quick intermission before they were right back to their river dancing. I tossed and turned for hours before falling asleep. When I awoke the next morning, I fought the urge to get up and message him a quick 'good morning'. I wanted to wait to speak to him until he was in front of me. Face to face and not over text messages. I knew the next few days would be absolute hell. I knew I needed to prepare myself for them to drag on with no clear end. Even while knowing this, I failed to do so.

I spent the afternoon sitting quietly at my desk clicking a pen and bouncing my leg while I stared at the clock. My mother had always told me that I needed to learn patience because patience is a virtue. I couldn't help but wonder where all my moral standards had gone, especially since most of them had been drilled into me since the moment I learned to speak. If I had to say it aloud, I think I first noticed it slipping away when I told my parents my first lie. What was it, you ask? Let me lay out the scene for you.

My mother and father came into my bedroom together. I immediately knew something was wrong as they'd hardly ever stepped foot into my room separately let alone together. I was sitting comfortably on my bed reading; A Single Man, and fawning over George and how absolutely cute I'd imagined him to be when they sat on either side of me. I folded the corner page of my book and shut it. *Did a relative die?* My mother rested an open-palmed hand on my thigh and began to speak. "Sweetie, you know you can talk to your father and me, right?"

Oh, here we go. I suddenly became very aware of what was happening. 'The talk', but not the one that normal little boys and girls get. *I'm getting the uncomfortable talk.* I looked around my room to find anything else to focus on. My frantic eyes completely skimmed over any sign of hope I'd held onto. Not even my poster of Liza Minnelli could save me this time. My entire body was frozen and when my dad put his hand on my other leg it didn't help the situation. This was awkward and I closed my eyes to wish it would go away. I peeked them open, no luck. They were still sitting next to me with their hands on me in what they thought was a comforting way. I set my book down in my lap and decided to listen to what they had to say. Not because I wanted to hear it, but because I needed them to get back up and walk out of my room so that I could crawl back into my own little world that consisted of me and Christopher Isherwood.

"I know I can come to you." I obliged them. I had to. I could hear the clear distress in my father's voice when he spoke next.

"Are you a homosexual, Rick?" His tone was quiet. I could

tell he was just as uncomfortable as I was, if not far more.

"If you are, you can tell us, Freddie, we won't be angry." My mother followed up.

I wanted to scream. I wanted to get up and run away and never stop. The deep internalized homophobia I'd already held towards myself flared up. I knew becoming defensive wouldn't help me in the slightest. I had never stopped to realize that telling them the truth then would have helped me in the future. I also hadn't realized that my silence was giving them the answer they didn't want. The answer that would make me the family disappointment.

"No," I said matter-of-factly. "I am not." I pretended to be appalled by the very nerve they had to question me. Though I was truly far more appalled by the fact that I had given myself away, even if I'd lied. They never had to ask me, they were being considerate of my feelings by sitting me down and telling me the information they already knew was true. They simply wanted confirmation. A confirmation I would never willingly give them.

The number of fixed dates my parents set up for me with girls after this was humiliating. I couldn't complain to anyone about it either. The only confidant I had was a small notebook I hid under my mattress in which I'd detailed every boring date. I'd tell it about the awful kiss we'd share at the end of the night and how I couldn't have been less interested. Usually, when you're out with someone, you're not as dense to the fact that they don't care. When I've gone on dates in the past, with someone I wanted to be out with, that's when I did my best detective work. Does this person seem interested in what I'm saying? Do they look me in the eyes when I'm speaking? Do they watch my lips a little too long? There are small things to look for. If I was out with someone who pulled half the shit I did, I'd never go out with them again.

I did the same thing for the next four days. Get up, get dressed, go to work, come home, go to sleep, repeat. Some days I'd be so lost in the clock that I'd forget to eat. Watching time go by soon became somewhat of a hobby that completely disinterested me. The next day was the day I had been waiting for. He even messaged me to make sure I was still coming. That alone made my heart flutter. I let out a deep breath as I clocked out for the day and made my way out to my car. I drove home and went inside to try and sleep. I could only compare it to waiting for Christmas day to come sooner as a child. How children waited in bed and stared out the window when they should be asleep. Becoming anxious when they remembered their mother saying that Santa wouldn't come because they were awake. That was the same feeling I felt that night. The small Irishmen came back with more oomph than before and made it nearly impossible to fall asleep.

After I stared at the blank white ceiling for what felt like forever, my body finally gave in. Though when it woke me again early the next morning, and I awoke exhausted, I was still excited. I got up and turned on the water to the shower. I stood and watched the steam roll out of the top until I snapped back to reality. I stepped in and let the hot water run over my incredibly tense shoulders — something I couldn't fight through my anxiousness. I was going to meet Santa today. By Santa, I mean that beautiful mystery man I'd gazed at on my computer screen for days. I couldn't wait to give him the list of what I'd wanted for Christmas; a list of questions that is and I had so many. What did he do for work? Where is he from? How long had he been online? How did he get his hair to do that natural-looking swoopy-doo as it was in his profile picture? Did he think I was as pretty as I thought he was? All on my list.

I turned the knob repeatedly to make the water scalding hot. I kept going until the point that I'd run out of hot water, only then had I decided to get out. I wrapped a towel around my body and prepared myself to stand in front of my closet for the next however many hours it would take me to decide on an outfit. To my surprise, it didn't take nearly as much time as I'd thought. I hadn't been sorting through hangers long before finding the simplest plaid dark blue suit. It even had a matching bow tie. I had never worn this suit. I remember not being able to leave the store without it. The different shades of blue over the plaid design were so visually pleasing and the blue bowtie was even prettier against the white shirt. I'd promptly dressed myself up in the suit and stared at my mess of a hairdo in the mirror. My hair could never look as good as his did, so I'd wear it the same way I did every day. Parted down the side and gelled back.

I tried to focus on my breathing throughout the entire drive to our meeting spot. The oranges and reds of the passing trees were particularly bright that day. The sky was blue and the clouds were fluffy. A day to remember, for the most part, a day that I'll tell people about one day. 'Oh, when did we meet? On a beautiful fall day in the middle of Central Park. The leaves fell in the most perfect way, just as they would in an opening scene to a romantic comedy starring Jennifer Lopez. The sky was a gorgeous soft blue and it was just windy enough to make your nose cold, but not windy enough to be inconvenienced'. I tried even harder not to get my hopes up when I walked through the walkways of the park, all the way to the Bethesda fountain. I'd always come here to read under the stairs on my days off work. I'd convinced myself that I might seem more appealing in a place that I'm comfortable. I was comfortable there. I even brought a book to read in case I got stood up. If I were to get stood up, I wouldn't want anyone else to know how pathetic I was so I brought a backup. I pulled out my back up and sat on the ground against the fountain. I'd decided to wait in a place I wasn't too fond of in case the worst happened. I waited for him there.

Chapter 3

It may have been around my second hour waiting for him that I began to curse myself for not bringing a scarf and gloves to keep my exposed skin warm. It was around the same time that I'd realized I left my phone at home, so I couldn't even check to see if he was going to be late. I frequently checked my watch and looked around to see if I saw him anywhere. I didn't. I gave myself some time to accept his absence and the fact that he may not be coming before I tried to relax, I needed to catch up on reading anyway. It wasn't until a little while later that I would look up from my book to see someone sitting next to me. The sun was bright and had originally blurred my vision, I was unable to connect a face to the outline of the head, but as soon as I was able to, I smiled.

"Listen, I looked for you. I didn't realize you'd be hiding by the fountain." His voice was so soft and sweet. It made my heart skip a few beats listening to him speak, I folded the corner page of my book and closed it. "How long have you been sitting here?" I quietly stammered and he watched me. *Say something, you idiot.* "What are you reading?" he asked me.

"The Bell Jar," I responded. "Or Shakespeare, whichever would make me seem more brilliant," I tried to appear confident in myself so he wouldn't see me lacking. He looked as if he wasn't sure about what I said. It made me frustrated with myself that I'd tried to be witty with him. "I'm reading The Bell Jar," I said again.

"A reader of banned books." He took my book out of my hands. "You've almost finished, when did you start?"

I didn't want to tell him that I'd just started in fear of him thinking I was smarter than he was. I didn't want him to be intimidated if he would be. So instead of answering his question, I asked my own. "Do you read?"

"Do you often change the subject when you don't want to answer?" He followed up with his own question. He'd caught me off guard, a part of me wanted to keep playing the witty game with him and ask another question. The other part of me, kept telling myself to just be me. Who cares if you're a bookworm?

"I started when I got here,"

"And you were here overnight?" Was he teasing me? Was that allowed?

I laughed a little and took my book back from him. "No, only a couple of hours." I made sure that my place was kept in the book before closing it again. "What do you do for work?" I pulled from my Christmas list of questions. I hadn't intended to seem so formal, but he made me nervous. After sitting in silence for a few moments it was clear to me that he was nervous too. It hadn't dawned on me that he may be pretending to be just as witty as I was. I let him have his silent moment before I spoke again. "I work at a bank." My abrupt interruption of the silence made him laugh at me. I couldn't help but notice how charming his laugh was and how it put mine to shame. Would everything he did feel perfect?

After he ceased his endearing outburst, he finally decided to give me a response. "I teach." Could his response have been more ideal?

"You teach," I repeated, almost as if I had to remind myself of the mere perfection that just came out of his mouth. I stole a free second to mull over what he said before I realized it sounded like I'd judged him with my silence. "You teach what?"

He smiled. *Oh, he smiled.* "The fifth grade."

"The fifth grade." I unintentionally repeated it.

"Just because you repeat what I'm saying doesn't mean you're actually contributing to this conversation," He was so bold to say so. Was he still pretending to be witty?

I let him bully me into my own stillness. Trying to think of something quick to say didn't come as easily to me as I'd originally thought. I thought back to his profile to try and catch the cat that had gotten my tongue. "What's your last name, Johnathon?" I received an immediate yield in conversation. The way he looked at me made me feel as if I was a kid who just got caught with a hand in the cookie jar.

"My father calls me Johnathon; you can call me Johnny." What a relief. I thought I would have gotten my hand slapped and sent to my room. "My last name is Burke." He got up from the ground and dusted off his bottom before offering me a hand. I was hesitant to take it, it must have been me not wanting him to feel the vibrations radiating through my desperation again, but I did. I took his hand and stood as well. It surprised me when he didn't instantly release me. Instead, he readjusted his fingers to snake their way through mine. A smile crossed my lips almost immediately and I looked down to hide it. I used my free hand to dust off my own pants and he tugged on my opposite one to walk with him.

We walked and talked side by side throughout the park. The entire time I found myself imagining what a life with him would be like. The extraordinary life of a teacher and a bank teller, 'Mr. Johnathan and Frederick Burke'. We'd both arrive home to our upper east side apartment around the same time. We'd order in from the greasy little Chinese restaurant a block away and sit together on the sofa while we watched romantic comedies until we were tired. We'd shower together and we'd go to bed together. On our same days off we would come back to the park to ride our bicycles around the whole perimeter. We'd share an ice cream cone from the vendor off the corner of Columbus Circle and then we'd go home to make love. Talk about moving upstate and starting a family, we'd adopt, of course. We would spend the rest of the day together, bickering quietly about what shape sconce we'd prefer to have in our forever home. He liked the older antique-looking ones and I wanted something more elegant. On our next day off we would grocery shop together. We'd happily walk hand in hand down the aisles of the grocery store without any care in the world of who saw or what they'd say. We wouldn't even stop long enough to hear their chatter. We would walk home after instead of taking the train or driving and we would simply enjoy one another's company.

Aside from envisioning our entire life together, I'd worried if he knew what was running through my mind. I also wondered that if he knew would he think I was a psychopath? I could only hope that if he one day found out. He would lightly tease me about it and call it a day. It's the polite thing to do when you find out someone fantasizes about you, isn't it? Acknowledge it and then pretend it never happened. Shrug it away as most people do with their unwanted problems. That only raised more fears for me. Would I become nothing more than an unwanted problem because I got too excited? Was my excitement so strong that he could sense it? I immediately looked down to make sure I wasn't showing it in a way that was unwelcome, at least so soon. Why was I being so hard on myself? If he doesn't like me, he never has to see me again, right? It would turn into a horror story that he would tell his friends about. The man who got too excited on a first date and he'd conveniently leave out the part where I basically worshipped his photograph for virtually two weeks. Though if he was courteous and asked me, I would tell him the truth and he wouldn't have to tell his friends a bad story. Instead, he could tell them that he met a man who really liked him and who thought he was a tall glass of water but it didn't work out.

Daydreaming as we walked made time go by so fast, I felt I'd just stood still while the world around us moved at hyperspeed. When I came back to reality he'd taken me back to my car, though he didn't try to say goodbye and rush away as most would after a bad date. He stood and proceeded to talk to me. Did he actually enjoy himself? It was at this point that I'd found myself not even paying attention to what he was saying, I watched his lips move yet heard no words. His lips looked like clouds and I just wanted to perch mine onto them. I wanted to float with him at his level. What would he do if I gave into myself and kissed him? Would he kiss me too? Or would he be upset? I'd never become so interested in someone in so little time. Before this very moment, I'd listened to every word that came from his mouth. He seemed to be comfortable enough to tell me about what felt like his whole world, and I ate it all up. I felt bad for not giving him as much to work with as he'd given me. My attention was recentered on him when he spoke directly at me.

"Frederick," He spoke to me like he'd known me forever.

"Johnny." I tried to be coy. He didn't have to try any harder to get me to notice him, he had my attention. This was the first time he was quiet during our entire date. I'd be lying if I said it didn't make me nervous. He looked like he was trying to say something important. He looked absolutely perfect in the afternoon sunlight. "Yes, Johnny?" I answered him again. I tried to let him know I wanted to know what he had to say. I looked down at both of our feet. Didn't I read somewhere that when you're with someone, if you want to know if they like you or not, just look at their feet? If their feet are pointed at you, they like you. I hadn't realized but my feet were pointing straight at him too. My mind didn't need much time to fall in love with Johnny before my body followed suit.

"Cat got your tongue?" I teased him.

"I don't know how this could possibly happen, Frederick," Thank God, he finally spoke, I thought he was having a stroke. "I think I'm falling for you."

I believe now would be a good time to name the three little river dancing Irishmen who've made a comfortable living in my gut. What do you think of Barry, Declan, and Knox? I felt the wind get knocked out of me. How could I have led myself on to believe that this man was so far out of my league when he clearly feels the same about me? I had to remind myself to breathe, or I think I'm the one who'll have the stroke. Do I admit to him that I feel the same way? Is this a cruel joke? If I didn't tell him the truth now would Declan, Barry, and Knox help me through the heartbreak when he inevitably left? Either way, I didn't want to find out, so I chose honesty.

"I feel the same way, Johnny." Happiness was a feeling I'd hardly experienced until this moment when I was ambushed with nothing but it. Before I knew it, his soft clouds were perched on top of mine. It would have been so much more romantic had my lips not been frozen from the chilly breeze. I only wished I had the nerve to kiss him first when I'd wanted to, and I'll regret not doing just that until the day I die. When we parted, though I didn't want to, I thought it would be a good idea to end the date before I got too carried away and started to explain how I'd let my imagination run wild. If I ruined this now, I would hate myself forever.

"Why do you drive a car around the city?" He broke our

sweet moment. *Back to reality.*

"People on the subway are weird." Was the only answer I could think of. I didn't want to come off cloud nine completely just yet.

"It's New York… people are weird." And I laughed at that. I happily climbed into my car and turned on the heater. He came over and opened my door again. He offered me the sweetest kiss, on my cheek, and I accepted by leaning into it. "When can I see you again?" The most important question he'd asked me all day. I couldn't wait to see him again and I hadn't left yet. I was happy to have known that I didn't get myself worked up for nothing. I was even happier that I didn't build this up to be more than what it was, the relationship did that all on its own. I wanted to give him an endearing answer. I wanted, even more, to give him a witty answer so that I could fulfill our false witty banter.

"Is tomorrow too soon?" That's not what I wanted. I wanted him to come home with me now, and never leave. 'Just stay. Get in my car with me and we can go look at apartments together'. Thankfully I'd grown accustomed to filtering what I said. If I said everything I'd thought, he'd never have agreed to meet me.

"I'll bring dinner," He closed my car door and I left him there. The only thing I could think of as I watched him out of my rearview mirror was… *I have to wait all damn day tomorrow to see you?* Hadn't I waited for him long enough? Almost two weeks with a few extra hours while I'd waited at the fountain. Putting a label on the amount of time did nothing for me but make me frustrated. It felt like I'd waited a lifetime to meet him and now that I had, I found myself craving his presence already. Though I wasn't quite psychopathic enough to turn my car around and go back. I'd let him suffer just the same as I had to.

Chapter 4

Our relationship from then on seemed to develop like clockwork. In a span of just a few months, it had evolved into something incredibly intimate. Our intimacy wasn't limited to physicality, it was also emotional. We began to spend every available moment together without growing tired of one another. I spent most of my time lying around on Johnny's sofa, or on Johnny. How could I have known a stranger I found on the internet would cure everything that was wrong with me in one fell swoop? Including my seasonal depression. After a couple years of happiness, I wouldn't have a care in the world. I'd come to know Johnny as everything he was, and he was lovely. He's a lot quieter than he originally came off, which settled my nerves knowing he was pretending to be just as witty as I was back then. We'd later had a good laugh about it. Not everything I had imagined would happen had happened yet. We didn't have an apartment on the upper east side together and we weren't married, not that it was legal for us to get married yet. Same-sex marriage wouldn't be passed in the city until July of 2011, though it wouldn't stop me from hoping at the time we'd be able to. We hadn't talked about children or moving upstate when we were old, but we did discreetly hold hands in the grocery store. It was then that I had started to notice how reserved Johnny was with his feelings for me in public, though I knew it wasn't true, it felt as though he was embarrassed by me. Every once and awhile I'd get ill will about it and mention something to him. If we were in public, he'd go on to mumble about how I knew he loved me and that we could discuss it later. Later never happened and I hadn't wanted to bring it up again.

It came to be that time again when Johnny would come home from work, and I felt like a dog waiting for its owner to fill its food bowl. I sat up on the sofa and watched the door like the hound I was, when I heard the keys turning in the doorknob, I felt like I had waited an eternity for him to come home when in reality I had only been lying there an hour. I hadn't bothered to change out of my work clothes, because I knew if I only waited long enough, he'd undress me instead, and I'd be lying if I said I wouldn't prefer it that way. I couldn't help but to undress him when he walked in, with my eyes, of course. Not a day went by that he didn't walk through that door looking absolutely amazing. I was never sure if he'd always chosen to dress up for work or if he only started wearing suits to work when I started staying over more. Was he just trying to impress me? That ship had sailed long ago, he hadn't needed to do so. But I didn't want him to stop.

"You look comfortable," he'd immediately teased me. "If you stare at me any longer, you may burn a hole right through me." He simply smiled and leaned over to kiss my forehead.

"I am comfortable." My body didn't need permission to lean into him, it did that on its own. I reached around his torso and leaned back into the sofa, having his body so close to me felt like we were two puzzle pieces coming together. It was completely perfect.

The sound he'd made when I pulled him to my level was nearly romantic, the smile he gave me afterward sealed the deal. He relaxed after a few moments and let the weight of his body melt against me. If I wasn't comfortable before I definitely was now. "Have you been home long, Frederick?" He spoke to me in the softest tone, I could have died and gone to heaven just then. He trailed a hand down my back and into the back of my jeans, he grabbed and squeezed my bottom. I didn't have a chance to react before he kissed me with his luscious pink clouds.

"Long enough," I mumbled against him and moved away just enough to brush my lips over his. "Long enough to feel like a dog waiting for its owner." I learned quickly to speak exactly what I thought when I was around him. He'd pressured me to until it was a natural occurrence, just as I pressured him to hold my hand when we were out. It wasn't because I felt needy, it was because I craved his touch. I wanted him to touch me, and I needed him to feel every crevice and mark every curve of my skin as his own. My entire being ached for him in every way. He looked at me just then, it felt as if he knew my mind was wandering elsewhere. My mind wandering off into deeper territory happened often, though I always listened to what he was saying, I continued to daydream about him. It didn't matter if he was right in front of me, or on top of me in this case, Johnny consumed my thoughts and self.

"What are you thinking about?" he asked me finally, after searching my eyes for answers of his own. Once he asked, he went back and forth between staring into my eyes and watching my lips.

"Sex," I said blatantly, which technically wasn't a lie.

Johnny laughed a bit. "Were you?"

I nodded. He didn't need to know I spent most of my time indulging myself in my own fantasies of him and I together. "Technically."

"I see," the way he looked at me sent chills down my spine. "Sex with me, I hope." And with that comment, I hit his shoulder. As if he had to ask if I ever wanted anyone else. How dare he assume that. My arousal at that point had been diminished into nothing, just a thought. I watched his eyes, trying to gauge if he was being serious or not.

"Of course," The expression on my face must have told him how offended I was before I could verbally express my opinion. He let my bottom go and removed his hand from the back of my jeans. I could only assume he felt how displeased I was with the comment. "Your sister, Charlotte, called today," I said. I realized that I wasn't the only one unhappy with a comment being made. I'd never met Johnny's family before. I was his best kept but still known secret. Everyone knew we were dating, yet he'd still kept me hidden. He never spoke much about them, and they didn't contact him much in return. It sparked a burning curiosity inside my chest whenever something so small was mentioned, though I dared not ask. His eyes looked broken when it was brought up, his composure would become lost and it would feel like we were in public. "She invited me to her son's baptism, Johnny, in two weeks" I let him see a small smile, I was just happy to be invited. "Can we go?" I had been so excited simply to be acknowledged by his sister. I assumed she hadn't known who I was, I answered her call solely seeking validation for myself.

I saw the hesitation in his face, he didn't want to answer my question, but he did out of obligation. Not only to me but to his new nephew. "If that's what you want," I could tell by his new tone that he was frustrated. He was sad.

"I want to meet your family." I reached up to his face and held his cheeks with a soft grip. "I want to actively be in your life." I was practically begging him for attention at this point and all I got in return was a simple nod at first. We shared eye contact for some time before either of us spoke again. It felt like the longest silence that had ever been between us when we were not asleep. His hesitation went further than his family, there were still somethings he held to himself. He didn't accept himself and I knew this. I went in for a kiss to reassure him that he wasn't alone and he opened his mouth to speak.

"You are my life, Frederick." His voice was nothing louder than a whisper. I knew he was sincere by the way he looked at me when he said it. The sadness in his eyes said it all, they said even more when tears welled up over those big, beautiful blue irises. I had never, during the time of our relationship, seen Johnny cry. I had grown accustomed to believing he didn't know how to, I knew he'd had a rough life, I wouldn't know just how rough it was until after we'd married. What I did know at that very moment was that I didn't like the dejected image in front of me. My heart ached for him, I wanted to consume him so that he could feel just how much I adored him. I wanted to make him feel just as wonderful as he made me feel, but I didn't know how to fix this. He closed his eyes and hid his face in the crook of my neck. I knew he was still crying even when his face was buried into me, I knew it was my fault.

"Sweetheart," I said to him, I waited only a few seconds for any sort of response. Deep down I knew I wouldn't get one. "I love you, Johnny." I held him tightly, giving him the loving embrace I thought he needed, in that moment. We stayed in that spot on the sofa for hours. I quietly listened to him cry while quietly hating myself for making him cry at the same time. I was almost waiting for him to cry himself to sleep. It had been nothing but silent tears for what seemed like forever. I couldn't help but hold resentment for my words, I hadn't known something so simple could turn my significant other into a puddle. He was a mess. He was my mess, mine to clean up. I pulled the blanket off the back of the sofa and spread it out over his back. I did my best to show him I cared for him. I did my best to make him feel comforted. The consistent weight of my lover lying on top of me was comparable to a weighted blanket, hot and comfortable. It felt like home to have him so close.

"Freddie." He finally broke the silence after some time. I was too scared to speak to him, I hadn't wanted to make him feel worse. He propped himself up over me and rested his weight onto his forearms. His face was red and his eyes were puffy, though it seemed as though he wasn't trying to hide that from me. He watched me intently, almost as if he was trying to force himself to form words. "I've been thinking for a while now-"

Oh my god, he's dumping me. That had to be it, I had finally screwed everything up with my impulsive comments. "Johnny, please, listen to me, I hadn't intended to hurt your feelings — it was stupid — I'll do anything—" I began to stammer like an idiot. My eyes desperately searched around the room for something to hold onto. After everything, he'd finally had enough with me. I'd always been frightened that he'd wake up one day and realize he was too perfect for me. Those fears were forgotten whenever I was with him. He'd made me feel so good that I was never able to think of anything else, there wasn't anything else to think about other than he and I, now he was leaving me. I'd lived and breathed his name for so long now, what would I do without him? I'll be alone again. I'd have to watch It's A Wonderful Life alone on Christmas. Who would assure me that watching romance comedies on repeat when you're sad is normal? My chest was tight, I could go straight into a panic attack if I'd allowed it to happen. Any minute now and I'd turn into a blubbering mess. "I don't want you to go—"

"I want you to marry me, Frederick." He had nearly laughed at me. He probably thought I was nuts. He pressed his thumbs

under my eyes and wiped away the tears that were about to fall.
"You're so silly." He placed a gentle kiss over my lips. All while
I was still trying to process the words that came out of his mouth.
Marry him?

"Johnny, it's — It's illegal—" I stammered some more.

"Marry me, Freddie," he pushed stray hairs out of my face
and back into place. The thought of marrying Johnny had crossed
my mind far too many times to count, I'd never imagined the
thought had also crossed his mind. I frantically nodded and
brought my lips up to his. Our kisses were fervent and needing.
He ran his hand around my face and tangled his fingers through
my short hair. It was amorous.

He moved his body off of mine and I let out a short huff of
breath when he pulled his lips away from mine, *where was he
going?* Then he picked me up like it was nothing, I may as well
have been a feather floating through the air. He was strong and
attentive. Our lips found each other again. It was where they
belonged, after all, against each other. I hadn't cared where he
was taking me so long as he went there too. My legs slowly
slipped out of his grip and met the floor, within seconds my body
was pressed against his bedroom door, soon to be our bedroom
door. My head instinctively tipped back against the wood as his
clouds found their way to my neck. Nothing was more arousing
than Johnny pressing against me, kissing my neck. I could
positively die just now. Instead, I wrapped my limbs around him.
My own fingers intertwined through his longer hair and grabbed
the back of his shirt. "Please don't stop." I could have sworn it
was a thought inside my own head, it hadn't dawned on me that
I'd said it aloud until Johnny smiled against my clavicle and
nipped my skin.

"Wasn't planning on it, thank you." He was so polite, now

was not the time for politeness. Especially not with a newly formed erection pressing against my jeans. I felt a whimper escape from the base of my throat. I hadn't known I could sing soprano. Only during intercourse, I presume. Johnny took me to The Met to see 'La Bohème' on our third date. I secretly always wished I could sing the high notes of Giacomo Puccini. The show was delightful. Not that I'd focused on it entirely. He held my hand the entire time. How was I supposed to focus on anything but him? By the time my mind was brought back to the present, I was partially undressed, and my chest was being kissed. I often wondered how he became so experienced with his mouth. How many other men or women had felt his clouds upon their own chests. I let myself sigh, a soft moan of encouragement as I tried not to think myself into such holes, especially when there was a good chance that he'd enter mine tonight.

It didn't matter how distracting he was, I was unsuccessful in saving myself from my own thoughts. I began to think about his sister and his nephew's baptism. I wondered if his family would like me at all. I hoped Johnny wouldn't let his family come between our relationship. Then I began to worry about where he thought we'd get married and why he asked for my hand. It was illegal for us to be married in New York, where would we go? I'd always imagined a dream wedding in the public library on fifth avenue. I also imagined I'd be friends with Barbra Streisand and she'd attend the wedding. I suppose that's why they called them dreams. How cruel would it be if I woke up one day and my sweet Johnny had been nothing but a dream? The universe would do that to me, my own mind would do that to me. My attention was brought back to reality when he nipped my shoulder, presumably to get me to refocus on what he was doing. He was often aware of how my mind tends to wander.

"Frederick, Darling," he breathed against me. There was nothing more endearing than his breath on my skin. I lifted my head a bit to acknowledge he was speaking to me. "Anxiety and intimacy don't belong together in the same room,"

Thanks for calling me out like that. "Who's anxious? Not me." *You're such a liar.*

"Float back down to earth, Freddie. Off your shrinking cloud. Let me catch you," His words were perfect. "I'll always catch you."

With that, I allowed myself to listen. He wrapped his arms around my torso and lifted me ever so slightly off the ground, enough to move me to his bed and lay me onto it. I watched his body become even with mine as he'd crawled over me. There would never be a time that I wouldn't give myself completely to this man. I relaxed entirely and focused solely on my fiancé, which I continued to do until I fell asleep next to him at sunrise the next morning.

Chapter 5

Our 'I do's' had come and gone in the blink of an eye. We'd traveled out of state and had a ceremony, just us two. It hadn't taken longer than a week for our lives to change. We promptly signed a new lease on a larger apartment on the upper west side near sixty-eighth street. It almost looked over Central Park, however, if I truly wanted to see it, I could walk down the hall opposite my apartment in the building and look out the window. I'd almost missed Johnny's smaller apartment, it was far more familiar, this one wasn't familiar enough. Our wedding wasn't everything I'd imagined, Barbara Streisand wasn't there, but Johnny was. I could have never imagined in a million years I'd find someone as charming as him. I could have never imagined I would find someone who was more than willing to stay with me as long as he has, more than that, someone who was committed to me until death would do us part. It had been so long since I'd believed in more than anything that I would be all right.

I had lost my faith in humanity years ago on a day when I was walking home from work, another reason I now drive everywhere. A co-worker of mine and I had become close. We worked near one another most days and I often confided in him; he was a younger man working as an intern over the summer. I thought we were friends but when he found out I wasn't into women, he grew distant and hadn't wanted to converse any more.

I hadn't intended on telling him, not because I was into him, but because most people didn't approve. He found out while we went out to lunch. He constantly attempted to partake in casual dating gossip around the workplace and I just wasn't into that. He'd point out how sexy a woman walking down the street was and proceed to catcall her. I'd done my best to keep my comments on the matter silent, however, his actions thoroughly bothered me. I'd start to tell him it wasn't appropriate and it was degrading to women. He then began to tease me and call me a feminist, that if I stood for women's rights, I must secretly be a woman. I responded to him with 'So what if I am?', something he hadn't taken so lightly.

"'You're a woman?" he'd scoffed at me, absolutely disgusted with the very thought of it. I simply shook my head, it wasn't true. I don't identify as a woman.

"No, a feminist," I had said. "So what if I am? Women and men are equal, why do you believe the woman you catcalled two minutes ago is anything less than yourself?" She wasn't. The woman was beautiful, she exuded confidence as she walked down the sidewalk. She deserved to be told how beautiful she was. She didn't wake up this morning to be sexualized as she went about her day.

"So, you're a homosexual, then?" he'd asked, though it was said more as a statement. The way he looked at me, I knew our friendship was over. He was revolted by the idea alone, how would he accept me when he knew what he'd asked me was true.

My silence, to him, gave him everything he needed to know. He didn't say a word to me, he simply turned and walked away. I had never feared the opinion of someone other than my parents, nor did I care to. I knew I was gay, I knew who I was and I knew I had never accepted myself. How could anyone else accept me when I couldn't accept myself? I didn't eat lunch that day, I'd had a nervous feeling in the pit of my stomach until he'd left work. I was a fool to assume I was safe once he'd left. I should have asked someone to stay with me, but I didn't, nor had I thought too. I remember being lethargic by closing time. I couldn't wait to curl into my bed. I closed the register for the evening and shut off the lights, then locked the door. It was dark outside, but I could see the entrance to the subway with the help of the dim streetlights. The distance between me and the entrance seemed miles away, farther than normal. I felt cold and for the first time in forever, scared to walk home in the darkness. So, I ran. I started to run to the subway. The subway meant safety. There were other people on the subway. There were policemen who typically waited in the halls late at night.

I wish it were simple and I could only say 'I got knocked out, I don't remember what happened' or perhaps nothing at all because I was killed. I wish they had killed me. I wish I hadn't spent a month in the ICU. I wish I called out of work that day as I'd planned to. I wish I had done something differently to stop that moment from happening, but I didn't. I couldn't. Things happen in life for a reason. He knew I took that subway home and he waited for me with his father. There was no one to help me. I was beaten within an inch of my life, but they wouldn't let me die. They wouldn't let me fall into unconsciousness, they wanted me to feel everything. Every kick, every hit, and every swing of their bat. Over and over until I was lying there bleeding, barely breathing, but alive. Alive and suffering. Alive and feeling. But I won, didn't I? I wanted to die there, but I am still alive today and I am married to the man I adore, which means that they lost. I was left with scars on my face and body, constant reminders of what had happened. The same year I met Johnny, I had the smallest amount of hope being 'fag bashed' wouldn't have been the only thing to happen to me that year.

I stood in the hallway of our apartment building, staring out the window, down into Central Park. I watched people walk their dogs and ride their bicycles through traffic. I turned my head and looked over my shoulder just as a hand rested on it. "What are you thinking about?" Johnny asked me, he leaned closer and kissed my temple, right below a scar on my face, conveniently. "You've been out here for quite some time," he continued. His smile made me forget all the bad things I was thinking about, quite literally. I forgot where I was for a single moment.

"I was watching people walk their dogs," I said to him. He lightly tugged on my shirt as a way of saying 'come back into our apartment' and I didn't think twice before following him. "Johnny, what should I wear to your nephew's baptism this weekend?" I trod lightly. "Can we go shopping?" I was teasing of course.

"I didn't know we had an extra few hundred dollars lying around after all we've spent on this place," he teased back. "You can shop directly out of our closet."

"Mm," I hummed, the smile on my face told him everything he'd needed to know. "Our closet," I repeated back to him. He closed our door behind us and locked it. I felt safer behind closed and locked doors, especially after recent memories began to resurface. I sat down at the bar in our kitchen just as our home phone began to ring. "Our first phone call in our new apartment as a married couple," I fawned as I'd picked up the phone. "Hello, who is this?" I answered happily and waited for an answer.

It was silent for what felt like minutes just before. "Hello, Frederick." Johnny's mother? My initial thought was *how did she get our number?* and my next was *act cool, Johnny doesn't need to know.*

"Good afternoon, how are you today?" My customer service skills were immaculate. I hadn't known why she would be calling and I wasn't about to allow her to speak to my husband. *Oh, my husband.*

"I'm well, is Johnathon around?"

"No, ma'am," I kept steady. I am not a good liar. I never have been.

"That's okay. I called to speak to you anyway, Frederick," she said, she sounded so sweet. *How condescending.* I smiled anyway.

"How nice of you, just to chat?" I asked, I like to talk.

"I don't think it's a good idea for you to... Attend our family's baptism celebration this weekend, Frederick." Her tone was definitely not sweet any more. It was cold. I didn't understand.

I fought through a short pause, I tried to find words. "I was invited." I responded, I glanced over to my husband and immediately looked away again. I didn't want to draw attention to myself or my phone call.

"My daughter was so sweet to do so." Where was this going? "It's just not a good idea for our family to see you with Johnny."

"I don't understand." Johnny was my husband. What was happening? There was an exasperated sigh. It sounded overly dramatic and frustrated.

"I don't want the family to see you together," she said again, there was a pause. "I don't want your relationship to influence the baby."

"He's an infant." I was quiet. Whispering at this point.

"I mean, exactly, right? He's just an infant!" She continued, every word like a dagger in my chest. "You shouldn't be putting those ideas in his head at such a young age. I knew you'd understand." But I didn't, I wouldn't. "You're so easy to talk to. Give my best to Johnny."

"Wait — I—" It was too late, she hung up on me. I placed the phone back onto its charger and stared at it. I finally understood why Johnny had kept them from me. I finally understood why he was so sad when they were brought up. They hated me. They'd never met me and they hated me. They don't want me to be with Johnny, didn't they know how much I loved him?

"Freddie, who was that?" He picked up the phone before I ever had the chance to stop him. "How upsetting. My mother was the first person to call us on our new phone in our new home." He attempted to make a light joke out of what I'd said before. "What did she want?" He hung the phone back onto its hook and leaned over the opposite side of the bar, so we'd make eye contact. I didn't want to answer that, I just wanted to swim in his deep ocean eyes for hours. "Frederick?" he asked again after I'd been silent for a few seconds.

I hesitated. "She asked me not to come to your nephew's baptism," I said quietly and immediately tried to make up for the truth. "It's all right, though, I probably have to work that day anyway." The smile I gave him was entirely forced. I met him halfway and pecked my lips onto his. "I'm going to get the last box out of my car." Code for, *I'm going to go cry in the stairwell for thirty or more minutes, so you don't see me.*

After a day like that, all I'd wanted to do by the end of it was take a long, scalding bath and melt into a puddle to become one with the water. It was days like these where I'd heavily considered going to therapy. *How would that work?* How do I know I'd be getting a therapist who would accept me? I tried to keep myself from letting her words sink under my skin, they hit me as hard as a fist. Had she wanted to hurt me? Was that her intention? If only she knew how much her words could affect someone's self-esteem, my self-esteem... Johnny's too. Destroying anyone's self-esteem would hurt them far more than physical abuse. It made me wonder just how awful his childhood was. It drove an even deeper concern through my very soul for

Johnny now. Was he okay? Was he keeping his deeper feelings from me? And did he think it was protecting me if he was doing so? How was I supposed to protect him from his family when I couldn't even protect myself? All I knew in that moment was that I felt as though I had to worry for my safety again, not only mine but Johnny's too. Her words circled my head like a forbidden merry-go-round, I wasn't allowed to ride it and I wasn't allowed to stop it. It seemed to have only brought back some of the horrible memories I had repressed. I began to think back to being beaten, back to people leaving, spitting at me and calling me names. Every word she said was like a kick in the gut, so much so that it felt like she'd reopened past scars. I felt like submerging myself into the tub and letting myself inhale the water. There were only two things that stopped me from acting on the feeling. One; my wonderful husband was asleep in the next room, and it would be selfish of me to let him find me like that. Two; I watched a documentary on the Discovery Channel about the worst ways to die — drowning was in the top three. They said that it didn't matter how desperate the drowning person was, they didn't inhale until they were on the verge of losing their consciousness, at that stage, there is far too much carbon dioxide in the blood, your body essentially forces you to take a breath. When your first involuntary breath happens, most are still conscious. The doctor who was interviewed about this looked like he was going to be sick. He said that it would be unfortunate for those still conscious as you would feel yourself suffocate; it would feel like you were burning from the inside out, it was pure torture. Then he proceeded to talk about how 'the very process of drowning makes it harder and harder *not* to drown'. Aside from not wanting to burn from the inside out, I wouldn't want to wake up and not see Johnny's face. If everyone was right about me and about religion, I wouldn't want to wake up in a fiery hell, just to burn from the outside in this time.

46

After I nearly fell asleep in the bathtub, I decided it was time to go to bed. I let out the water and I made sure I was completely dried before slipping into some comfortable pajamas. I put the bathroom back in order and crawled into bed next to my husband. I could go to sleep peacefully with him next to me. I knew I was safe with him. The only place I'd have to worry about drowning would be in my dreams or possibly my emotions. It calmed me immensely to feel the warmth of his body against mine once I'd nuzzled up to him. I pulled the comforter over the both of us and pressed my face into his back. He smelled like old books and grass, an odd combination but I wasn't sure what else to expect from a fifth-grade teacher. I always assumed he started rolling in the grass as soon as he showed up for work. I closed my eyes and inhaled deeply, taking in the scent before allowing myself to relax against the pillows. It felt weird sleeping in a new bed. It felt even weirder sleeping in a new room. I knew I'd have to get used to it at some point, so I tried to force myself to sleep for the night. Somehow, through my mind's racing thoughts and the new distractions from our new apartment, I was able to doze off and I didn't dream about drowning. I dreamt about how much easier our lives would be if I were a woman when we married, how much easier it would be for Johnny and his family if I were able to be normal for him. I could bear children for him, take care of him and his family when they were old. All the easy things a typical wife would do as if I didn't do them already. The only issue they had was what was in my pants, right? I may as well have dreamt about drowning.

Chapter 6

I met Johnny's family nearly a year later while attending the wedding of a mutual friend. He was horrified when his family walked up to him, but he smiled anyway and embraced each of them as if he had no issues at all. I sat and watched him from the bar while the bartender poured our champagne. I could never be as strong as he was. I would have actively avoided any sort of contact with them, family or not. You don't treat people the way they had treated him and I. I picked up our flutes of champagne and approached the group of people surrounding my husband. His mother, father, sister and nephew, all standing around him like the start of a bad meeting that could have been sent in an email. I stood nearby and watched them interact with each other before I walked up to them and held out a flute of champagne for Johnny.

I offered him a simple smile. "Who's this?" I asked him as though I hadn't known. I couldn't help but notice the absence of his wedding ring when he'd taken the glass from me. He wasn't one to wear it in public, but he had it on when I left to get the champagne.

"Hello, Frederick," Johnny's mother, Vivian, greeted me. "How have you been?" she asked me as if the last time we'd spoken she wasn't a blatant homophobic bitch.

"I'm well, thank you." I was polite despite not wanting to be. "Johnny and I have been very—" It didn't take long for her to interrupt me.

"Johnathon, this is Johnny's friend Frederick," she said, referring to Johnny's father. "Remember, we've told you about him—"

What have you told him about me?

I received a short smile from the older man. "I have heard a little about you. You recently moved in with my boy Johnny, yeah?"

Did he know we were married?

"Yes, actually, we got—" Interrupted. Again. This time by Johnny.

"He's, my roommate." The words were quick to come out of his mouth and even quicker to stab me in the back. Roommate? What the hell was happening. I felt like I wasn't being heard. I felt invisible.

"They've lived together for nearly a year now, they're really good friends. Johnny was so sweet to put him up in that big expensive apartment of his." His mother stabbed me again. "That teacher's salary does him well."

"What are you talking about, we're not—" The next person who interrupted me was going to get throat punched.

"Yes, well, it was nice meeting you." His father shook my hand. "Maverick? Was it? Maybe I'll stop by sometime." And he was gone along with the rest of them.

I corrected him anyway. "It's... Frederick, actually..." I said, dejected. I couldn't bring myself to look at Johnny. I couldn't believe the conversation I'd just heard. I also couldn't tell if I wanted to cry or hit someone. The frustration, or possibly just anxiety was tight in my chest. I had never been so embarrassed to be in public, nor had I ever been so ashamed to be in the same room as my husband. The thought immediately occurred to me that he may feel the same about me. He might have been ashamed of me too. That was why he introduced me as his roommate and not his husband. That was why he didn't stand up to his family. My husband was ashamed of me too. Though I wasn't perpetually ashamed, only in that moment. I didn't want to cause a scene in front of everyone but I could feel the uproar of stares looking my way. It felt like there was a giant spotlight overhead and everyone was laughing at me, the fool who thought his husband was different and had more respect for him than that. When I looked up, there was no one looking, just Johnny, which was validation enough that I was being stared at. His stare had the power of a hundred stares. His stare also had the power to make me feel guilty for being angry. He knew he'd hurt my feelings and that's why he was silent.

He reached for me and grabbed the sleeve of my suit in an attempt to pull me near to him, I promptly swatted his hand away and shook my head at him. "Don't touch me." And I left. I went home and I left him at the party by himself. It hadn't hit me until now that I didn't have friends, I didn't have anyone to talk to except Johnny. I was devastated, how is it that the person who hurt me most was the only one I wanted to talk to? But how am I supposed to tell the one who hurt me everything as if they aren't the one who caused my distress? I didn't, I suffered in silence. I went home and I packed an overnight bag. Which may have been dramatic, but I couldn't imagine wanting to stay in the same bed as the man who broke my heart that same night. It was impulsive but I left, and I didn't leave a note. All I could think about was how hurt I was and how angry I was with Johnny. Did he even want to be married to me? I had always been understanding and I'd always defended him. When would I be understood? When would I get to be defended?

I checked into a room down the street from our apartment.

I'd contemplated not going back home all night, I considered going to my father's house to vent to him. Not that he would understand. My father had been insufferably dense ever since the day he and my mother had 'The Talk' with me. I didn't have to tell them what they thought was true, I could have denied it forever and even married a woman to make them happy and they would have still known it wasn't who I wanted to be with or what I wanted out of life. I could have sucked it up and married our neighbor Josephine. We could have had a loveless marriage with three children who would end up unhappy because their parents divorced twenty years into their marriage. I could have been in upstate New York by now and had the easy wedding at the public library with Barbara Streisand. All of which I would have lost in the divorce because she would have had a better lawyer than me, which then had me thinking, would Johnny have a better lawyer than me? Of course he would, he made more money than me. Nothing in our apartment belonged to me, he didn't even have to have a co-signer on the lease. Johnny owned everything, what did I own? Clothes and the yogurt I bought last week from the grocery store on my way home from work. If I left him, I would have nothing, which overall was a compelling argument to stay. As was still being in love with him, despite how often his actions hurt me. Was this something that I could potentially get over? Or would I dwell on it every time I was alone. I tend to dwell on the past when I'm alone, I understand it's a toxic habit, not only for myself but to those around me, but I still do it. I dwelled on being beaten after work, I dwelled on being uninvited to his nephew's baptism, I dwelled on Johnny taking off his wedding ring when we left the house, on my parents not being active in my life because of who I was, and probably not in any future child of mine's life too, on the way Vivian treated her son and on my husband introducing me as his roommate. I dwelled a hole through the wall in my hotel room.

Part of me regrets the damage I'd done, not only to my mental health but to the private property I'd just destroyed and couldn't afford to pay for. I stared at the hole all night, the great ramification of my bottled-up anger. Therapy didn't sound so horrible in that moment; I may have needed far more than that when my husband gets a bill for room repairs. I dozed off sometime the next morning, just as the sun started to peek through the curtains. I couldn't bring myself to go home yet and face reality. I couldn't bring myself to go home and face my husband, emotionally and quite literally. I didn't want to look at him or think about him, but my mind was cruel. Even if I ultimately decided to leave our marriage, I'd have to undergo many years of therapy for the emotional turmoil I would have put myself through. By the time I'd allowed myself to fall into a deeper sleep, I was woken up by knocking. I only hoped it was the couple's headboard in the next room banging against the wall. Of course, when I opened my eyes well enough to focus, I'd realized it was the door. Someone was knocking on my door.

Chapter 7

"What did you say?" I asked my husband. The look on his face was one that I'd never wanted to see again. His eyes drooped when he was sad. More so when he cried. I had only seen Johnny cry a handful of times and each time it was my fault. This time, by far, was the worst. I didn't know how long I would have to make him feel better and I assumed the doctor wouldn't know either. You will always see situations like this in movies, so and so has six weeks to live, and then so and so goes on the 'adventure of a lifetime' and then dies before their six weeks are up. Well so and so shouldn't have stressed themselves out and maybe they'd have lived longer. I didn't plan on traveling the world, my world was there with Johnny. My world was Johnny. Perhaps he could simply hold me in his arms for six weeks, brush my hair back with his fingers, and whisper to me that everything would be okay. I wasn't scared of dying, I was scared of leaving him alone. I'm comparable to a guide dog, if I leave, he'll get lost, either physically or mentally. Who will save him from himself? Who will save him from his family?

"You have cancer, Frederick," he repeated to himself. How many times would I make him say it? Enough. Until I believed it.

"Okay," I said, though I wasn't convinced it was really happening. The sound of the door opening and closing again was music to my ears, anything to pull me out of this moment of pure emotional chaos I felt I was in.

"Acute Myeloid Leukemia, A-M-L." The doctor spelled out for me. "We were unable to determine exactly how long you've had it, after a few tests we'll know more," he said. "Currently there is no cure, however, you can forestall the harsher effects with chemotherapy, you may qualify for stem cell transplants as well."

More Spanish. I looked to Johnny for translation or possibly some silent moral support. Was I going to die?

Johnny listened to the doctor and kept himself composed while he spoke to us, I assume for my benefit rather than his own. "What's the survival rate?" He was asking the harder questions. The ones I wouldn't ask myself, at least not in front of him. "Will he be okay?"

"A-M-L grows a lot faster than other forms of leukemia, the average male over the age of twenty has a twenty-six percent survival rate, most don't last more than five years if it goes untreated," he explained, Johnny was quick to interrupt him.

"Treatment? You said there wasn't a cure."

"Currently there isn't," he continued with a soft tone. "However, with proper care — with proper treatment," he corrected himself. "You could add years to your' life and live happily."

"How can we possibly live happily when he's going to die?" I had never heard my husband raise his voice in the entirety of the time I had known him, he didn't even raise his voice at his students. He was reserved and sweet, he wouldn't want to hurt anyone's feelings, but in the moment, he looked as though he would kill the doctor.

"I understand there will be immediate feelings of loss, Mr. Burke, no one lives forever, I know it's an unfortunate way to part from one another, but he's not gone now. He still has time, all I can suggest is that you live your life as fully as possible."

This doctor was in full just live as if you're in a tragic romantic comedy mode. He even used our last name in an apologetic way, am I the main character of this movie? Could it be one with many sequels? The longer the better, it could be like Harry Potter, long and never-ending. I wish our life together could be long and never-ending.

My doctor continued to try and comfort my husband. He stayed in the room with us and explained all of our options and where we should go from that point. I'd have to spend the next five weeks in the hospital for treatment, I didn't want to stay in the hospital. Though who wanted to be in a hospital ever? Johnny agreed continuously to things the doctor was explaining, treatments and in home care. All I could think was, can we even afford that? I knew I couldn't. Thought after thought, worry after worry soon came to a simmer, I wouldn't allow myself to boil over, not in front of Johnny. Not right now. It wasn't long before I started to ask myself if I *should* do the movie ending, spend every waking moment with my husband. Quit my job, travel, start a family. I wanted children with him, I wanted a dog and I wanted a domestic life with him, leaving now would be too soon. Leaving him ever would be too soon.

The conversation between my husband and doctor began to sound like gobbledygook again, I wasn't following what they were saying and I felt overwhelmed with the confusion of not knowing. I watched between them for quite some time before I dared interrupt them. "I don't want to stay here," I blurted. "I want to go home, I don't want to spend the only time I have left in a hospital."

"Frederick, what are you saying?" Johnny was angry. I couldn't tell if what I said made it worse or was simply the source of his anger. "Of course you'll stay here, you need help."

"And do what? Sit here alone without you?"

"No, I — You — You just have to." Was all he was able to

come up with on the spot. "You need help. I need you to stay. For me, if anything."

"Johnny, I want to adopt children. I want to get a dog and I want to see the day I'm allowed to marry you in the library on fifth avenue. I can't live with you if I'm living the rest of my life in a hospital room," I explained to him. "I don't want to go through treatment for something that could maybe let me have more time with you."

"Freddie, you're not being reasonable!"

"Don't yell at me, Johnny, please, take me home." I knew he wasn't okay. His posture bent and he grew quiet. I didn't know if it was a quiet acceptance or just more anger. I slid sideways out of the white sheets and sat on the edge of the bed. "Johnny, baby, we can go home. If I'm going to die, I'd prefer you not to watch me get sick and wither away." I grabbed his hands. "Take me home, Johnny." I kissed them. "Take me home."

The intimacy we'd had together was indescribable, the harder the moments were, the deeper the intimacy was. We didn't have to touch to know we'd crave the other's presence, their voice, their smell. The drive home was silent and tense. It lacked the intimacy we'd have carried if that day hadn't happened. It lacked the need for his presence and touch, I wanted to sleep.

Earlier that day, I had nearly reached his work; I was bringing him lunch, after he'd forgotten the one I packed him. I lent him my car because he was late and I took the subway to see him. I was exhausted and I was dizzy, I hadn't even made it to the office to check in. I hit the ground like a ton of bricks, it hurt and then it didn't, then it hurt again when I woke up in the emergency room and my husband wasn't with me. How bad would it hurt Johnny when he wakes up in our bedroom without me? Would he move on, or would he go into a depression? Would he kill himself? Am I foolish to think I mean that much to anyone, that they'd commit suicide if I was gone? Perhaps not foolish, but selfish to think so.

He helped me out of the car and into the elevator of our apartment building. I had a certain feeling of helplessness rush over me, I knew I'd be taken care of every moment of the day. Suddenly, Johnny not leaving my side gave me anxiety. Not because I didn't love him, but because it would be a constant 'don't move, I'll do it for you' kind of closeness. A constant cheek-to-cheek in my own personal hell kind of close. Any sort of closeness to him should be at least mildly appreciated, however, I was afraid it may borderline on overbearing. I didn't want to become frustrated when he was simply trying to help me. I didn't want him to stray from me because I didn't appreciate him enough. I didn't want him to stray from me because I was distant and sick or because I drove him away. It weighed my mind as those thoughts crossed it, would my husband act unfaithful to me because of this? Not just because of the leukemia, of course, but everything? Would everything drive him away from me?

I was led into our apartment and sat in a chair by the television. Johnny stewed a cup of tea and brought it to me, then promptly wrapped me up in a blanket. I quietly laughed at him and nuzzled down into the seat. I laughed a bit more when he turned *It's A Wonderful Life* on the television. Making light of this situation wasn't going to be easy, living the situation was going to be worse. I sipped the tea I'd been given, and Johnny poured himself a glass of scotch then sat down next to me. This would be the only time we'd watch this movie in silence instead of reciting every word together.

Chapter 8

Who was knocking on my door? The only question I could apparently think of except who was knocking on my hotel room door, when no one knew I was there and I didn't order room service? Could the hotel manager sense the wall was damaged? Would they kick me out? I stared at the door confused, a second knock startled me and then a muffled voice. I couldn't quite make out what they said or who it was, so I got out of bed and answered the door. To my surprise, my husband stood on the other side. How could he have known where I was?

"I bet you're wondering how I found you,"

Uh, yeah, I am.

"You used our credit card for the room charge, Freddie," he spoke with a tone that made me incredibly nervous. Was he mad at me or was he sad I left?

"You could have called." I began to fidget with my wedding ring in an attempt to focus on anything but him. Seeing him only hurt my feelings more. "I'm just your roommate, after all, Johnny. There's no need to check up on me, I'm doing just fine." I felt him stare directly into my soul, I almost wanted to cower away. Johnny didn't scare me, he'd never given me a reason to fear him, though his feelings were intense and not exactly expressed well. He'd never raised his voice at me, he'd never hit me. His emotions were far worse than that, they were bottled up inside of him waiting to escape. He'd been a dormant volcano for so many years, the next eruption would be unpredictable.

"Is that why there's a hole in the wall?" He looked from the hole, back into my eyes. "Freddie, you can't run from me, we're married. We have to talk about this."

I nearly laughed at him, instead what came out was an awkward huff. "Married behind closed doors, roommates in public."

"Freddie, come home, I need you to come home. I love you don't you know that?" he'd practically begged me. I didn't want to go home. I didn't want to go back into our apartment that had been tainted by his roommate accusations. I didn't want to only be loved behind closed doors. I could have broken down and cried in front of him now. Tears threatened to come loose and then all I could think about was how lucky I should feel that I have someone who loved me at all. A man who loved me enough to find me when I was upset and ran away. Then all I could think was how toxic I was to myself and that if I let myself forgive him so quickly, would he continue to think I would forgive him for anything he did? Would he walk all over me and continue to think I was a pushover?

"I know that you love me." Was all I could think of to say to him. Did I know he loved me? Is that something I knew for sure or something I continued to tell myself to feel better? Everyone aches to be loved. Everyone wants a pair of eyes to meet their own. Everyone wants to come home after a long day of work and feel the breath of their one and only against their lips right before they kiss. I didn't want to lose that feeling of being loved, even if it was only from the comfort of my home. I didn't want to lose Johnny, but I also didn't want to feel like I was nothing more than a roommate for the rest of my life.

"Do you still love me?"

With that I cracked. I couldn't control the emotion that

spilled out of my eyes. Of course I still loved him. "Of course I still love you." The sounds that came after that were nothing but blubbering gibberish. I'd felt confused and betrayed, but I didn't want to hurt him. I didn't want him to feel as though I'd give up on him so easily. If only his dating profile all those years ago said 'Emotionally unavailable and has daddy issues', maybe I wouldn't be in this mess. Although I'd still potentially be alone.

"Will you let me take you home?" He asked me. There was a long silent pause between the two of us. "If you don't want to go home, we could stay in the hotel room and have sex instead," he's really hitting on me right now? "At least then we can tell the manager we were getting frisky and accidentally fucked a hole right into the wall,"

"You can tell him that story anyway, it doesn't need to be true for it to be said. You know how to lie, don't you, Johnny?" I would prefer being alone right now. Perhaps I'd potentially feel different after I'd slept more than three hours. I handed him my bag and walked out past him into the hallway. "I'll go home," I said. "But not because you want me to. It's because I want to." even though I didn't want to, and it absolutely was because he wanted me to. He didn't need to know that.

I didn't feel differently after I'd slept and I didn't feel differently after a week or more had passed. I continued to feel hurt every time I'd hear or see him. He tried to apologize and he'd tried to be romantic. I'd almost started to feel bad when I'd continuously shut him down. I slept in our guest bedroom and stayed there if I knew he was home. I'd made sure to wake up before him every morning to make him lunch for work, then slip back into the room to go back to sleep or at least pretend I was asleep when he came in to kiss me goodbye for the day. When he started leaving his lunch behind after he'd left, I only could assume he knew I'd feel so awful that he wouldn't be eating that day that I would bring it to him. He was right, though at first, I didn't need to see him, I'd be petty and drop it off in the main office with a note that said from your roommate or something equally as upsetting. He may not be aware of how much he hurt me from my lack of expression towards him, at least that's what I began to assume. After some time, I'd started to miss what I'd lost. I missed the closeness of being with somebody, I missed waking up to his groggy smile, I missed how soft his hands were, I missed the sex. I went to sleep that night thinking I should allow myself to feel closure with the hurt he'd caused me.

I woke up the next morning particularly more aroused than usual. I made Johnny his lunch earlier that morning and went back to bed again. I didn't sleep, I couldn't fall back to sleep because I wanted him. What better way to make up from a fight than with sex in a place you're not supposed to be having it; in an elementary school. I rolled out of bed and dressed myself. Johnny must have been subconsciously sabotaging my plans. *He didn't forget to take his lunch today.* Perhaps he wasn't purposefully leaving it behind to see me and I'd made it all up to make myself feel better. It wouldn't be the first time it'd happened. I wouldn't let it stop me, I grabbed an apple out of the refrigerator and left. I hadn't completely gotten over what Johnny did, but I was in a place where I was ready to work through it. After all, I'd decided I didn't want to divorce him. Not over something that could be rectified if he would just tell them the truth. I wish I could simply go back to daydreaming of our future together instead of dwelling on what we were now. God forbid, I dwell another hole into our wall.

Driving into the school's parking lot only brought me flashbacks of my own time in elementary school. Eating lunch alone, having no friends and oh yeah, having a crush on the fifth-grade teacher. Not much has changed, only now I'm married to the fifth-grade teacher. I always thought marriage meant you never had to eat lunch alone again because your significant other would replace all the loneliness. Your significant other would be your best friend. Boy was I wrong. After I thought myself into a hole, I started having second thoughts about rekindling my marriage. The second thoughts turned into third and fourth thoughts as I'd approached Johnny's classroom. He was having a conversation with a woman, and I didn't want to be rude and interrupt, so I leaned against the wall outside and eavesdropped instead. Their voices were quiet, however just loud enough that I could hear exactly what was said.

"I'd love for you to come over sometime to meet Frederick," that was obviously Johnny kissing my ass even when I wasn't around. "I think he would like you. You could watch those… romance movies together." *Romance movies? They were called romantic comedies and they were awesome.*

"Romantic comedies," the other voice corrected, *thank you.* "I'm sure he's nice." There was an uncomfortable amount of silence between them that stretched all the way out into the hallway, even making me uncomfortable listening to them. "Are you seeing anyone?"

"Am I seeing anyone?" he said as though he was confused by the question. The conversation wasn't exactly a conversation, it was blatant flirting. That woman was flirting with my husband. Suddenly I hadn't felt so bad eavesdropping on their discussion.

"Are you dating anyone?" I didn't have to see her face to know she was flashing him some sort of hookerish smile. She was probably flipping her hair back too. Too bad for her, Johnny was gay.

"Well... I — not exactly—" he was stammering like an idiot. He was an idiot. *Tell her you're married.* The woman giggled at him. *Yeah, I know he's charming. But* don't let him fool you, he's also an asshole. Johnny's play at innocence was entirely charming and I'm sure he knew it and used it to his advantage.

"Great, it's a date then. Saturday, we're having drinks at The Plaza. Six o'clock, don't be late." Is this how all women get dates nowadays? By making plans so fast that the reciprocating end doesn't have a chance to tell them they're married. I couldn't listen to any more of it, I hadn't cared if it was rude at that point. I walked in, nearly storming in. I was angry and I wanted to see who it was that just asked my husband out on a date.

It was my worst nightmare. A leggy blonde with pretty blue eyes and silky hair. Just the type of woman Johnny would have married if I hadn't come along to ruin everything. I'd only be lying to myself if I said she wasn't beautiful.

"Don't bring your roommate. Just yourself." Her voice wasn't above a murmur when I'd walked in. Johnny looked mortified, probably wondering what I'd heard. The leggy blonde flashed me a smile. It wasn't hookerish at all. Her teeth were perfectly white and straight. I looked like a trash can compared to her. "Hello, I don't believe we've met." Was she talking to me? "My name is Elizabeth Kaige, you must be the new science teacher," *You wish I was the new science teacher.*

I begrudgingly shook the hand she extended to me and forced a small smile. "Would you excuse me? I would like to have a private conversation with Mr. Burke." I tried to stay happy and formal so she'd continue to believe I worked there instead of thinking I was the roommate. I closed and locked the door behind her as she left and glanced over to Johnny, waiting for him to speak first. Would he tell me about Saturday night or keep it from me?

"I hadn't expected to see you," he said with a short smile. "Did you bring me an apple?"

Yes, I brought you an apple.

"No." I took a bite out of it.

"Oh." He closed his laptop and sat back in his chair. "Have you come to eat lunch with me, then?"

"No." I most certainly did not, I came to get laid and I wasn't so sure I wanted it now.

"Have you come to yell at me?" I shook my head at him and took another bite of the apple before throwing it away. "That was wasteful," he said to me. *Wasteful?*

"How private is your classroom?" I asked him. "When is your lunch break over?"

"Oh, I see. I get it. You're going to murder me. With a half-eaten apple?" I laughed a little and he smiled at me. "I miss that sound. I miss you, Freddie."

"I came to seduce you on your lunch break," I said, followed by an awkward pause. "But I don't know if it's too late to do so or when your kids will start coming in from recess," I explained and it didn't matter. Within seconds Johnny had crossed the room to me and his hands were grabbing my face and his lips were kissing mine.

"Lunch ends in twenty minutes," he said between kisses. His hands released my face and searched down my body. I didn't know if it was my inner touch-starved demons that worsened my arousal or the fact that we pursued intimacy in a public setting but I wanted him with every fiber of my being.

"Fore-play for five minutes, sex for eight minutes and the last seven for cuddling." The kisses I gave him were sloppy, I didn't care much about them as I didn't want him to know I still held passion for him. I wanted him to think I was in control for once, I wanted him to know I wasn't a pushover.

"Don't threaten me with a good time—" And clothes were sent flying throughout the room. He was quick to jump at the chance at intercourse, did that mean he wanted me too? Or was Elizabeth not putting out for him? I wasn't either, it would have been easy for him to stray from our vows the last few days, I wouldn't have noticed if he came home smelling of another's fragrant perfume, or… Cologne if he chose to sleep with another man. I could clear all of my own drifting thoughts now if I only asked him. I was scared it would push him away. I was scared it'd make him angry with me as I'd been with him. The thought of hurting Johnny was a foreign concept to me, if only it had been to him. I wish he'd think about what he was about to say before he said it.

All of my thoughts were jumbled, each coming one after another and another until there was absolutely nothing to think about except my husband pulling me into his naked lap. Our bodies readjusted comfortably on their own and mine accepted him in me as though it'd been a missing piece all along. I was unable to think of anything at this point. All my worries and protests floated away into the clouds and all that mattered was how good Johnny felt. His lips against my skin and his hands gripping my body in all the right places. After so many days of self-loathing I could have gotten a high from the affection I was receiving, it was as if Johnny was the heroin, and I was well overdue for a drug high. I got my hit and then took one more, then another and another until I was blissfully unaware of my marital issues and the world surrounding the two of us. I was blissfully unaware of anything except our synced breaths and each time I'd said Johnny's name. I was trying the best I could to be quiet, though I'm not the quietest in bed anyways, I didn't want to draw unwanted attention to his classroom. I'd tried instead to focus on my breathing, something that was stolen directly from my lips when Johnny kissed me. It wasn't long after that I'd moan out his name one last time in the middle of his kisses before releasing a long overdue and much-needed token of appreciation, all over his abdomen. My body collapsed against his and I felt happily exhausted.

"I'm afraid we won't have time for those cuddles, Freddie," his breath was hot against my cheek, he placed short kisses over my face, making his way back to my lips. "Put your clothes back on."

Way to make me feel like a cheap prostitute. I climbed out of his lap, my balance was a little wobbly at first but I'd promptly picked up the articles of clothing off the floor and dressed as I did.

"Freddie." He composed himself. "Are you mad at me?"

"I'll see you at home," I finished dressing and slipped out of the room. I pushed my hair back out of my face and felt as though I could cry. All the thoughts that floated away came crashing back down to my level at light-speed. *You're not good enough for him* and now added with *You're a whore* and even *He'd have preferred Elizabeth.* I got back into my car and watched the clouds pass by out of the sunroof. How much more pathetic could I possibly get? I desperately wanted to be angry with him. I wanted to march back in there and yell at him for not telling me about his date with that woman. I wanted to tell him that he hurt me and I wasn't ready to forgive him. What would he say to me if I told him that?

'Well, you could have fooled me, Freddie, especially after being balls deep inside you a few minutes ago'. Even my mental image of Johnny mocked me and told me I was wrong. Was I wrong? Was I wrong for feeling upset? *Am I overreacting?* Or had I not overreacted enough? Should I have been angrier than I was? How could I possibly be angry with him when all I really wanted to do was go back into his classroom and crawl back into his lap. Recess had likely ended by now and there wouldn't be time to pull him aside to talk to him, so I'd gone home instead. I went into our apartment feeling so different than when I'd left earlier. I felt filthy and felt as though I'd been used and thrown away. It was no one's fault but my own, though I'm almost positive I could have found some wavelength in my being in which I could have blamed the feeling on Elizabeth. Elizabeth with the legs, Elizabeth with the smile, Elizabeth with the hair. Elizabeth, who has a date with my husband on Saturday evening at six o'clock. I hated Elizabeth.

Chapter 9

My eyes burned with sleep every day for a month. I only wished leukemia was the worst of my problems but of course, it wasn't. I began seeing a therapist during trying times and I'd only hoped I could talk Johnny into going with me. He'd been distant and overwhelming all in the same breath. I'd often wondered if the two of us would make it out of this alive or if the stress alone would push me straight to my death, something I expressed to my therapist frequently. I hadn't wanted to seek comfort in a therapist, I'd tried to talk to Johnny. He didn't want to listen, at least it felt as though he didn't. He'd become quiet and reserved and would ultimately leave the room or the apartment in general. He'd be gone for hours and come home looking like he'd been run over by a semi-truck, then crawl into bed as though nothing had happened. Part of me wondered if he was still spending time with Elizabeth, another part of me wanted to forget I'd ever met her and forget that Johnny went out with her three Saturdays ago at six o'clock. He'd never mentioned a word of her to me and he lied that day about where he was going. I contemplated following him, but what was the point? I knew exactly where he was going, and if I followed him, it would have been my fault I didn't trust him. I didn't know if I didn't trust him or did, I did know that I was jealous. Jealous when he came home with a smile on his face because I figured she told him a joke and he laughed, jealous when he came home and smelled differently than when he left, jealous of the elderly woman who sits down on the park bench below our apartment, who hopefully doesn't have nearly as much to be jealous about as I do, who is probably a normal woman and doesn't have a care in the world. I wish I didn't have a care in the world.

"Freddie." The number of times he's interrupted my internal monologue. "I have some applications we need to fill out. Some for New Jersey, California and New York. The sooner we fill them out, the sooner we get an in-home interview."

Why would we want someone to give us an in-home interview? So, they can tell us we belong in the looney bin? Let alone have a stranger into our home willingly, this was New York City for Christ's sake. "Applications for what?"

"For adoption, Frederick. You asked me about it last week, did you change your mind?"

"You remembered something I asked you last week?"

"It was more of a comment, you said you wanted to adopt a kid." The smile on his face had something of an innocence that I had a hard time saying no to. I couldn't possibly tell him that I was scared a social worker would come in here to interview us and see something we didn't. When we got the report back it would say 'incompatible couple' or 'homosexual disasters'.

"I do… I want a kid. An older one, probably. One who hasn't had a good life or has had trouble getting adopted." If only I was brave enough to tell him that adopting a child now wouldn't do anything but slap a giant Band-Aid over our marital problems, unless he thought we didn't have any. Was all of this in my head? Am I bipolar? Or schizophrenic? Is this all something I created and none of it was true? Is Elizabeth even a real person or a figment of my imagination? It's become harder to differentiate what's been a vivid dream or real lately. Do I even have cancer? Perhaps this is all something I put together and I'm the one who needs help, *I needed to go see my therapist.*

"My mother is on her way," he set the papers aside. He should have opened the discussion with that, so I knew to leave. "We'll fill them out together when she leaves." Was that supposed to entice me to stay?

"Fine." I seated myself comfortably in my chair. I pulled my book off the coffee table and pretended to read it while I waited for the wicked bitch of the west to arrive.

"I asked her to be nice," as if that would help.

"If I had known you'd invited Satan herself over, I would have coordinated a nap around the same time." My eyes couldn't roll further into the back of my head. "Or drowned myself." I was never not nice to Vivian, but the thought of her made me want to kill myself. Actually, seeing her made me want to do so much worse. I glanced at Johnny, the sad puppy-dog expression on his face told me everything I needed to know about how he'd felt. It was just the kind of manipulation I'd needed first thing on a Sunday morning. "I'm sorry," I told him, though I didn't mean it. If anyone deserved an apology, I felt I did. Johnny wasn't the type of person to apologize for anything unless he knew it hurt you or if he was ashamed of it himself, he was often unashamed of the things he'd said or done. It would seem he had gotten the trait from Vivian, thankfully I woke up with just the right amount of cynicism to deal with both of them.

"That's the book you were reading the day we met." Did he think making small talk with me would make me any less aggravated?

"No," I said to him. "I was reading The Bell Jar." I remember everything from that day. It was arguably the best day of my life, something I could only hope was true for Johnny too. The whole day was romantic and I'd wished I could go back and live in the moment forever. Going back to that moment would erase our relationship, though. I didn't know if I was prepared for that to happen, nor did I know if I wanted that to happen. I wish I could forget the bad parts, but I wouldn't want to forget everything.

"Or Shakespeare," he said. "Whatever would make you seem smarter?" He smiled at me. Oh, he smiled. With a comment so small I remembered why I loved him. Why I love him, despite everything. Johnny was sweeter to me than I gave him credit for. I often allowed myself to become unappreciative of the man I had in my life. You only have so much time in your life, not enough time to spend half of it, not appreciating what you have. I appreciated him a little less when I knew the knock on our door was his mother. I appreciated him a little more when he placed a kiss on top of my head as he walked by to answer our door. It was moments like these that I lived for, the ones that make me incredibly happy before I remember; *oh yeah? I have cancer.*

If I hadn't known Vivian was coming over, getting a whiff of her cheap perfume as she walked through the door would have been a dead giveaway. If not the perfume, her voice. I like to think she was just as, if not more, annoying than Janice Hosenstein. She tended to sound like her at times too. It wasn't awful enough she had to come over, she came and made herself comfortable on the sofa across from where I was sitting. *Great, now I have to look at her too.*

"Freddie," Vivian's voice cut through the air like a knife. *Did it get colder when she walked in or was it just me?* "You look… Thinner."

I look thinner? Thanks? "Vivian." I smiled at her, genuinely because I thought my introduction was funnier than hers. "You've gotten fatter." And it was funnier. I could feel the icy stare digging into the back of my head, it could have only been from Johnny. I would not apologize, it was completely worth it.

Vivian's smile back at me was vindictive. Her eyes followed Johnny, who sat in the chair next to mine. "How's your friend, Johnny?"

"You know he's not just my friend, ma," He surprised me. I knew his mother knew about the two of us but I didn't know I'd ever heard him admit it. I smiled softly at him to let him know I appreciated what he'd said.

"No, no. Not Freddie. That woman, the one you brought to your father's birthday party last week. What was her name?" she looked at me, as though she was rubbing it in my face that he'd gone behind my back.

"Elizabeth." I looked to the floor, putting puzzle pieces together as she continued to tease me.

"Yes! Elizabeth, she's beautiful, Johnny. I brought her jacket back, she left it on the porch swing. You two seem close, where did you meet?" That woman was in her prime environment. She could have made a living bringing other people down, she was already so good at it.

"She works with me," Johnny spoke up finally. "She teaches special education in the classroom next to mine." He looked at me as though I'd believe anything he said. "We're just friends."

"Oh, I'm sorry, Freddie, did he not tell you he was going with her?" She knew he didn't. She knew that I was caught off guard and I wouldn't let her win.

"No, he told me." The smile on my face wouldn't last much longer. "I knew already. She is quite beautiful, isn't she, Vivian? Leggy, too."

"Incredibly beautiful. Johnathon just loved her. We all did, Johnny. You should bring her around more often." What an awful woman. "Why don't you invite her to dinner tomorrow night? We could all come over. You and I can cook, Freddie." If she smiled any more, her face could have frozen that way forever. She'd end up looking like that puppet from Saw more than she already did.

"Ma, I don't think that's a good idea—" Johnny murmured. He looked away from me and looked at his mother instead. If I saw his face, I'm sure he'd have a look of dread smacked all over it.

"We'll see you all at six o'clock, Vivian. Oh, how I'd love to cook with you." *Oh, how I would not.* I wouldn't be walked all over in my own home. I would not be the one who looked like a fool in the end of all of this and I would not be hidden from his family. Elizabeth would not take Johnny from me. I sat there quietly for the remainder of her visit. I sent his father a card for his birthday, if I'd known he was going to see him I would have given it to him to deliver himself. Why did he take her to the party? Why didn't he tell me he was taking her? I began to think of all the times in the last few weeks that he hadn't been home and wondered if he was with her. I wondered myself straight into an endless pit of worry that I was slowly losing my grip on my life. I was losing parts of myself, the best parts of myself and keeping the worst, as well as my sanity. By the time I'd centered myself enough to take more hits from Vivian, she was being led out by Johnny. I waited to hear the door close before getting out of my seat, the only thing keeping me comfortable now.

"You knew?" I couldn't look at him. How many more times would he do this to me before I stood up for myself?

"No," I responded quietly. "I didn't know." My palms were sweaty with anxiety and I looked around the room for an outlet, anything to focus on but the angry-rapid beating inside my chest. "I didn't know," I repeated. "But I didn't want to be told about my life inside my own apartment."

"She's just a friend, Freddie, I didn't want to take you to my parent's house only to be ridiculed all night." He kept talking. For what? Was he trying to talk himself out of this? Was he trying to make me feel better? He kept going and his words began to sound like gobbledygook to me, only now I didn't have anyone to translate what was being said. I stared outside the window and watched the clouds float by while he spoke, I thought about how slow they looked going by compared to how fast we all moved on the ground. I wish I could go to where time moved slow, up in the clouds. Where I'd have more time to process everything going on.

"Say anything, baby, please," It was as if he appeared in front of me. His hands were on my face, gripping my cheeks as though he was about to give me an unwanted kiss.

"You didn't take me because you were afraid your family would make fun of me." I pushed his hands away from me in order not to give into his oceanic eyes. "You didn't want your family to know you were married to a mess of a man. And a man in general." He didn't want his father to know he was a homosexual above all things, but I wouldn't stoop so low as to poke that wound, even if I vaguely did anyway. If I were a teenager, I'd hide in my room and blast sad Elton John songs into my squishy headphones. He was the only man who understood any gay's problems after all. Unfortunately, I was a married adult who now shared a room, while I could hide in the guest room and my parents knew not to bother me, Johnny would continue to push me until I popped. All I'd ever wanted was to be happy and in love, what romantic comedies don't tell you is that it only lasts for a few seconds before it's issue after issue. The movies don't show how many times he's going to make you cry and how many times he's going to make you hate yourself. They don't show you how the relationship ends. Only how it starts.

I wiped under my eyes before I'd had the chance to cry and kissed Johnny's cheek. I didn't have the energy to fight, it made me dizzy just thinking I'd have to continue the evening with an argument. I went to the kitchen and poured myself a glass of water, I'd need it in the morning after all the crying I was about to do to get myself to sleep. I knew I'd wake up and inhale the water like a whale. I brought it to our bedroom and climbed into bed. The wedding photo on my nightstand mocked me, it showed me a time of complete bliss. Something I didn't have now and it burned me on the inside. I felt the need to fix everything in only a second and I knew I couldn't. Everything was a constant stoke to the fire that was building inside, it made me wonder when my own volcano would erupt. I wasn't so worried about Johnny's any more, I was worried I'd say something or do something to hurt him just as bad. I never thought I'd stoop so low I'd want to hurt anyone, especially not Johnny, but I couldn't help but let the negativity of my thoughts roam wild. I felt betrayed by something I didn't know was actually happening. I did know that Johnny lied to me, but how deep was the lie? Were he and Elizabeth just friends? I knew he was insecure about himself, but was he so insecure that he'd ruin our marriage?

I went grocery shopping by myself the next morning in preparation for the evening. I wasn't going to allow Vivian to school me in my own apartment, in my own kitchen. Another part of me didn't want Johnny to have a chance to be alone with Elizabeth before I spoke to her. I didn't know if I'd confront her and blatantly ask what she thought she was doing with my husband or play dumb and ask elementary school questions like 'what do you think of Johnny?' and 'do you think he's cute?'. I never imagined I'd ever be in such an awkward situation. I never imagined my life would be so undeniably pathetic. I walked around the store with an empty cart, it would seem the universe got a kick out of my self-loathing, and placed lovers everywhere. Couples holding hands, couples kissing, couples picking out their vegetables together. Love birds all around me and I haven't even decided what to have for dinner yet. I could try to butterfly lobster tails again. The last time I'd tried to I was unable to finish. Johnny had come into the kitchen to help me, so he said. He ended up being nothing but a distraction and we ate apples and peanut butter for dinner that night.

I was standing in front of the sink in his old apartment over on fifth avenue and twenty-third street. There was a window behind his sink with pretty blue billowy curtains. I often stood there and did dishes just to watch out the window. The trees always seemed to be so green and behind the pockets of space without leaves, there was an old red brick building. I washed asparagus and lemons, then the lobster tails. The little feet on the bottom of the tails always creeped me out, they were like the spiders of the ocean. I didn't like bugs, especially not spiders, especially not sea-spiders, but they tasted so good. I would only buy the tails, I hated having to cook a whole lobster and then beheading the corpse. The tails were simpler to clean, anyway. I had just put everything into a colander and turned the water back on for a final rinse when I heard music in the next room, followed by arms that slithered around my waist from behind. Johnny made me smile, he was so charming. I leaned back into him and allowed him to kiss the back of my neck. It tickled and my laughter only praised him.

"I'm cooking dinner," I'd said to him, happily so. Just like a housewife. "But don't stop." I'd encouraged him and then laughed some more when he kissed my neck again with his soft,

soft clouds.

"So, you need my help then," his grip around me was welcoming and warm, he felt like home. "I could help squeeze the lemons," and one of his hands found their way to my bottom, he held me in place and squeezed my lemons.

"You can't have dessert, you haven't eaten your dinner yet." I'd teased him and it went downhill from there. We didn't have sex, try as he may have, it was more intimate. He turned me to face him and picked me up just enough so I could sit on the countertop. He stood in between my knees and watched my eyes and lips, he stood there and made simple conversation with me for what felt like only moments, but lasted for an hour or more. He spoke to me about things that worried him and the color of his bedroom wall as a kid. All I could think about was how no one else in the world could ever be so lucky as I was to have someone like Johnny. Now all I can think about is how lucky Elizabeth is to have someone like Johnny, after all the time I just know they're spending together.

I had to float off my reminiscent cloud for just a second as it was interrupted by an elderly woman asking if I could reach the canned tomatoes off the top shelf. Of course I could do that for her. I got my lobster tails and everything else I'd needed then left. When I got home I had to start cooking in order to finish by the time Vivian and the rest of her cult of homophobes showed up.

I stood in front of our new kitchen sink, looking out of our new kitchen window. The clouds would never be as fluffy and the trees would never be as bright. The difference between the windows wasn't the scenery outside, it was a difference of perspective. I wish I was still stuck in a daydream as I was back then, I wish Johnny would hug me from behind and kiss the back of my neck. I wish I didn't believe that tonight would be the end of my marriage, perhaps only if that's what I wanted it to be. I didn't, but sometimes it seemed to be easier to let go than to hold onto something that would never be the same as it was before. Would it be easier if I left Johnny? Would it be easier to let him go? Would it be easier on him if he didn't have to deal with me and my death sentence? I wish I could look out the window and see a rainbow at the end of the dark tunnel. I wish I could open up and let Johnny into the mess inside my head, I was scared. If he knew what I thought all the time I don't believe he'd love me, did he think the same? Would I love him if I saw what was really on the inside? What was really on the inside of Johnny? Lies and self-torture? Love and affection? Internalized homophobia towards himself and guilt? All of my own insecurities simmered up and started to boil over. There was no one to watch my pot while it boiled. I assumed Johnny would have taken the responsibility but he simply sat a wooden spoon over the top and walked away. He let me sink down into the bubbling water and I couldn't decide if I'd let him save my life this time or let myself drown instead. My daydreams had turned wicked after so many years. I used to daydream about life with Johnny, now I daydreamed about dying alone and divorce. If you could even consider it daydreaming, I often forget that nightmares can be dreams too. If Johnny and I ever separated, I wouldn't have anyone left. A weight would be lifted off Johnny's shoulders and I'd die alone in my studio apartment downtown. No one would care or know, my neighbors would call my landlord and complain about a bad smell after months and they'd break my door down to find my decomposing body, still by the window where I was sitting when I died from heartbreak.

I'd been ripped off another cloud and yanked back to reality when Vivian's voice echoed like canon fire through my kitchen.

I had just finished setting the table when she walked in and I couldn't be more thankful that I'd finished before she arrived, I only hoped it would cut everyone's evenings short.

"Freddie, you cooked without me! Is this your way of telling me I'm a bad cook? You're so bad!" Her laugh was more of a cackle and she was the only one who thought she was funny. 'I'm so bad', was I bad for protecting myself from two hours of 'Freddie, you didn't put enough garlic in the potatoes, I'll have to fix that' and whatever other complaints she'd have. Maybe her breath wouldn't smell so bad if she didn't eat so much garlic.

"I've been told you use too much butter." I offered her a half smile only. "It goes straight to your thighs, you know?" I believe women look stunning at any shape or size, but Vivian, she was not a woman. She was some breed of alien cow that Area-51 wasn't allowed to do experiments on because she was the only of her kind.

Then came the moment that ruined the entire evening, not that there was much left worth ruining, the leggy blonde arrived. She was even more beautiful than I'd allowed myself to remember. "I feel so embarrassed, last we met I took you for an employee. You're Frederick. The roommate." The roommate. When I die, my tombstone will read:

Frederick Burke, he was just a roommate.

I didn't dignify it with a response. I only smiled and pulled her chair out for her so she'd sit down for dinner.

"Aren't you going to get my chair for me, Freddie?" Vivian could have imploded in front of me and I would clap and ask to see it again.

"Your hands aren't broken, do it yourself." I was bitter and I wasn't about to apologize for it. I felt I had nothing to apologize for, even if Johnny disagreed and he did disagree. I felt the stare burning a hole through my skull. I smiled at him too. "Sit down for dinner, sweetheart." My voice floated over the tension in the room and sliced directly into his stare, even so I pulled out the chair for him so he could sit. I may not be towards Vivian, but I am a gentleman and unlike my husband, I was not afraid to show my affection for him in front of anyone. Especially not his family.

I placed food on everyone's plates, grabbing Vivian's plate last. I contemplated spitting in her butter cup, but I figured if I allowed myself to, I would be just as low as she was. So I didn't. "I melted low-fat butter for you, Vivian."

"Oh, Freddie, you didn't need to do that." Followed by a smile that only the Grinch could have, before he stole Christmas and his heart grew three sizes of course, it was yellow, bugs and all. Vivian's heart could grow three sizes and she would still be just as horrible.

"Anything to help my monster in law." I sat across from Elizabeth, who seemed confused by the situation yet still had the time to watch Johnny's every move. "Where's Johnathon tonight?" Not that I'd actually cared.

"He wasn't feeling well, he stayed home." Charlotte was Johnny's sister. She didn't have much to say, a true female version of him. Reserved. I quietly hoped she was nothing like her mother.

Too bad Vivian hadn't stayed home because she wasn't feeling well. That would have been the ideal circumstance. Johnny initially being honest with me would have also been the ideal circumstance. I sat there and pushed food around my plate, listening to them happily talk to each other in front of me felt like hearing that my husband had a completely separate life without me. It felt as though he was afraid to live our two lives together. In all reality, he probably was scared. He'd treated me like expensive china since we came home from the hospital, since I denied treatment. I wished he'd take me out of the cabinet and use me, I was not broken yet and if I did break, I wish he'd kintsugi me back together.

They all spoke to each other as if I were invisible. I may as well not have been there, I wished I wasn't there. I'd mumble something, every once in a while, when Charlotte or Johnny would mention something about how delicious they thought the food was. Johnny was specifically quiet and clearly tried not to make contact with Elizabeth in front of me, or maybe he was actually disinterested. One could only hope that was the case. I'd been fighting with myself in order to stay mad at him, perhaps it was time for me to lose that fight, or at least run away from it for now. I wanted to run away from it. I wanted to find a soft place to fall into, Johnny's lips for instance. I quickly turned away from him when I caught myself staring.

"Why don't we all go have a drink in the living room? We could play a game of Monopoly or something." It was bold of her to assume we had Monopoly. I can only imagine that a drunk Vivian would make me want to push her out the eighteenth-floor window far more than sober Vivian did. And Monopoly, could she have chosen a longer game?

"Ma, I have to work early. I don't think it's a good idea." Johnny must have known I wasn't comfortable with the idea, though I would have said something more along the lines of 'Do you think you need a drink, Viv?', he must have been trying to spare his mother's feelings.

"Of course, Johnny, that's all right. How else would you pay for your luxury apartment?" *Oh, the nerve.* If Johnny had spent as much time sticking up for our marriage as he did with his foot in his mouth a lot of our issues could have been prevented.

While they gathered at the door, I started to clean the table. I saw Elizabeth pull Johnny aside just out of the corner of my eye. It caught my attention and I'd tried to stay quiet so I could hear what was said between the two. Eavesdropping was suddenly becoming an unwanted hobby of mine.

"So, I was thinking." She pulled him off to the side of the room. "My parents invited me to my grandparent's cabin upstate," *Don't you dare go where I think you're going with this.* "I want them to meet you, Johnny." *What a slut.* If it wasn't the bedroom eyes she was looking at him with, it was her body language. The way she leaned into him and stared at his lips because she wanted something from him. I would know, I did it too.

"That's nice of you to offer," Was he playing awkward because he knew I could hear him? Or was he going to be honest with her instead? "Unfortunately, I won't be able to make the trip, I have to take care of Freddie. He's not doing well," He watched her, but not her lips, her eyes. *Take care of me?* I have never felt more like a burden. I can take care of myself.

"Doesn't he have other friends or something who could watch out for him?" She asked him. No, I did not. Johnny was all I had and I wouldn't let a leggy blonde with a hookerish smile take him from me.

"Elizabeth." He held her face. *Stop.* I couldn't look away from the disaster in front of me. Though, more so across the room from me. "Freddie is my... well — He's more to me than I've led on." *Say it. 'Freddie is your* husband'. He was quiet for far too long. He was holding her for far too long. It made me feel uncomfortable to watch, but I couldn't pull my gaze away from the eye-sore. "He's my spouse." *Fucking finally.*

Elizabeth laughed at him. *What the hell was so funny?* I could have cried. "You're so silly." What happened next *wrecked* me. I felt my world flash in front of my eyes and I couldn't unsee it. When she kissed him, I felt like everything I was afraid of was confirmed true. She didn't just kiss him, she was comfortable doing so. She was comfortable enough with him that she felt it was allowed. I didn't stay long enough to see what happened after, I made an escape out the front door and caught the elevator before it closed. The next thing I knew, I was trapped in the smallest of spaces with Vivian and Charlotte on the way down.

Hold yourself together, Freddie, just until she's gone.

"Are you all right, Freddie? Your face is all red, Darling." Her wrinkly finger crossed my cheek under my eye, I assumed to wipe away the tear that had betrayed me. "Is it Johnny and Elizabeth?" I was pulled into a hug that I couldn't escape from, it was brutal torture after the start of a war. Her clammy palms pushed hair out of my face that had stuck to my forehead and she spoke in a soft tone. "I'm so sorry you had to find out about them this way, but get real, Freddie." Her soft motherly tone turned into a condescending one once she'd opened her mouth and spoke. It was the longest elevator ride of my life. "You're a homosexual, Freddie. You chose a lifestyle that will cause you nothing except loneliness. You'll never find a real love, not one that will stick around. You should have known better when you tried to make Johnny the way you are too." I couldn't push myself from her arms quick enough. I let myself go and I lost. I cried in front of her and all it did was let her know that she won. "God can save you from your sins, Freddie. You and Johnny." She rummaged through her purse and pulled a small bible out. She extended it to me. "I've underlined some verses for you. You're more than welcome to call me if you need help reading it, I know it's hard to take in information. You know... with your condition?"

The ding of the elevator wasn't distraction enough. I should have left without dignifying it with a response. But I'm not as strong as I'd like to be. I snatched the bible out of her hand and held it up. "This? Your bible? It wasn't written by God. The ten commandments were written by God. Your bible was written by men, by over forty different men. The words you follow are based on preposterous laws written hundreds of years ago," I snapped at her. It felt good to let my pot boil over, it was a long time coming. My therapist must have called me a treasure enough times that I'd allowed my tank to empty itself. "And I don't have a condition, Vivian. I have leukemia." I exited the elevator before she had a chance to respond. I was in desperate need of some fresh air, anywhere that was free of the scent of last centuries Dior scrubbed straight from the scratch and sniff magazine and onto that old, saggy skin. A walk would do me some good.

Chapter 10

Somewhere in the crowded streets of Vienna or Paris, even Times Square, there are lovers dancing together in the midst of the chaos. Their fingertips would graze each other's skin and they'd swell into the intimacy between the two of them. All I thought about as I walked through Central Park was how happy they must be and how distraught they'd come to be. My own whirlwind romance had turned luckless in the blink of an eye. I couldn't tell if this was anything but a bad dream, and I just hadn't woken up from it yet. In my bad dream, I was trapped, freezing inside Johnny's wilderness and I was scared to return to our cave to face him. As I made my way back to that cave, I noticed an elderly woman sitting on the park bench, and I sat by her. This woman sat there nearly every day, I frequently saw her while watching people walk their dogs out the hall window. I offered her a smile and she rested a hand on my knee.

"You're troubled." Her voice was soft and sweet, it almost made me feel guilty I hadn't stopped and spoken to her sooner. I should have felt guilty, we'd lived in that apartment for a long while now. "Young man, what's the matter?" I couldn't help but love the woman already. I placed my hand on top of hers despite my insides screaming that it was 'New York and strangers don't talk to each other', which was clearly nothing but the stigma of the city.

"What's your name?" I asked her and looked her way. Her eyes were warm and intelligent, a wise shade of brown. "I've been awfully rude, I've watched you out my window, I should have greeted you."

"Shame on you for not doing so." She chuckled at me in a way that I would know she was teasing. "Harriet Dorsey. What's your name?"

"Frederick Burke." I watched her white curls blow in the wind. "Why do you come here?" I was curious who could possibly have this much time on their hands to come and sit at the parks for hours. I only wished I could do that. I used to.

"I met my late husband, Archie, here," She grinned at me and looked over at the street corner. "We ate our lunches here every day during our breaks from work." I watched her with green envy. How lucky Archie was to have someone so loyal to him, even in the afterlife.

"Could you tell me about him? If you don't mind." I wanted to hear her story. She squeezed my hand as though she'd known me forever. "Please," I quietly begged her for more. Someone needed to remind me that romance still existed in the world.

"I missed my train and was late to work, so I rode my bicycle that day. He was sitting here, right where you are now. I wasn't going fast, but he'd seen me and stuck out his foot to get run over. I felt so awful, I thought I'd hurt him." She laughed some and looked at our hands. "We met later in my life after his first marriage, we didn't have children, just the two of us."

Just the two of them. How perfect it must have been. "How did he... Go?" I asked her quietly.

"He had cancer and... We didn't catch it in time. He died in his sleep peacefully. I thank God every day that he didn't suffer." She let out a deep breath, I could tell it was hard for her to talk about. I wanted to tell her I knew exactly how she felt, say; *I have cancer*, but this wasn't my moment. It wasn't fair to her to make her story about me. I felt bad for asking anyway, but I kept going.

"So… Why do you come back?" She let my hand go and she composed herself. She took a deep breath of fresh air and let it out with a simple smile.

"Because I still feel him here, Frederick." It was that simple. She'd love him forever. "He told me that if he didn't make it, to meet him here for lunch every day. That he'd be here too, even if it wasn't physically." The way she spoke of him brought tears to my eyes. I felt her pain and I felt the unconditional love she had for Archie. Sweet, sweet Harriet and Archie Dorsey. The way she spoke of him made me feel ungrateful for what I had, or used to have. It made me question what I'd do when I went back up the elevator. "Frederick, what troubles you," she asked me again, though I didn't want to answer. What would she say to me if I told her I saw *my husband… A man…* Kissing a woman.

"My marriage isn't doing so well," I said simply and smiled at her again. She circled her hand in a sort of 'go on' gesture. "I don't know what is safe to say."

"If it's unsafe to speak of, why are you married?" *Don't call me out like that, old lady.*

"It's not that…" I sighed and readjusted, uncomfortable. "My marriage… It's — Well… I'm married to a man." I nearly cringed in expectation of some sort of lash out towards me. *Please don't throw rocks at me.* But she kept her smile.

"Do you love him?" *Simple.*

"Very much." I wouldn't make eye contact.

"Then what's so wrong with that?" I was surprised, it was shocking to me that she didn't need an explanation for acceptance. "Look at me, dear," and I did as I was told. "Don't let anyone… take away the love that you found, or the love that you think you found. Hold him close and love him as though

87

today will be your last." Where has she been all my life? She was so wise. I could sit here with her forever.

"I don't know if he wants me any more, Harriet." My voice was broken and wavered. What would I do if Johnny didn't want me? What would he say? How would he say it? I didn't want to go upstairs and find out.

"Don't let anything come between you, this man you love… If you care for him and he cares for you… It will just… Work. There won't be much else to it." She shrugged at me. The wisest woman I'd ever met and she just shrugged and said 'Make it work' as if it was the easiest task in the world. "You should let him in, it seems you're shutting him out, why?"

"I have leukemia." Tears welled into my eyes, a new common occurrence. I had been so focused on Johnny that I hadn't sorted my own feelings out about it all. "If I let him in, I'll only hurt him. I don't want to be just a memory to him… It's not bad yet, but I—"

"Frederick, cancer is only a death sentence if you let it be. Archie didn't wake up and feel bad for himself, he quit his job and spent the rest of his time enjoying life. He'd come to work at the news stand with me… We had a good time. Happiness cures doubt." If only I was able to explain everything to her without seeming like I was a mess of a human. After everything, she was still smiling and pushing through life. She was spreading joy, I even felt a little better after talking to her.

"Harriet, would you like to come upstairs for dinner sometime?"

"You're learning already, dear." It took her a little extra time to get her old legs standing, but when she got up, she leaned over and kissed my forehead. Something a grandmother would do. "You know where to find me," she said softly and picked up her cane. I watched her walk away from me until I couldn't see her any more. I looked up to the hallway window to our apartment and contemplated going back.

Going upstairs meant talking to Johnny. Talking to Johnny could mean so many different outcomes. Our relationship could potentially be over this evening. What if he looked at me and told me he didn't love me any more? *Oh my god, what if Johnny didn't love me any more?* Was I Johnny's cancer? The burden in his life that he couldn't shake off? Was he afraid of the consequences if he started chemotherapy to get rid of me? Something I was too proud to do; treatment. Something I didn't want to waste my time doing. Or was I only his death sentence if he let me be? Has he been happy with me all along and I was the one who stepped over the line? Happiness cures doubt, that's what she said. Could she have known that I was the problem holding our marriage back?

I prepared myself for an argument as I'd stood up. I didn't know what Johnny would have to say to me, but I knew I had to get some things off my chest. Whatever it was that weighed my heart down as I entered the elevator made me feel as though I would collapse on the way up. I was never a fan of confrontation, in fact, I actively avoided it at all cost. I missed the days I believed that Johnny would only be mine forever. All I wanted was a love that lasts, did that mean there was something wrong with me? Were my expectations for that love just too high? I could only hope I wasn't pushing Johnny upwards onto a pedestal of my own standards that he couldn't hold himself to. When I'd gotten to our floor, I stopped by the hallway window and looked out of it. It'd started to rain in the short time I was walking upstairs, was mother-nature trying to tell me something? That confronting Johnny would only lead to tears? Was I reading too much into this?

I stood by the door to listen and make sure everyone was gone before I entered. Johnny had cleaned the table and was doing the dishes. As I watched him stand there, the only thought that crossed through my mind was how domestic he looked with the little apron tied around his waist while he washed our plates. I quietly shut the door and closed the latch to lock it. I heard the water shut off in the kitchen, when I turned around, Johnny stood there drying his hands and watching me.

He offered a half smile as though he didn't know how I was feeling. "You're home, I was worried you wouldn't come back."

"We… Should talk, Johnny." And he sat on the bar stool to let me know he was listening. I looked him up and down for a moment. "If you take the apron off, I'll finish the dishes," I said. *Stop stalling*.

"You don't want to talk about the dishes, Frederick, you want to talk about Elizabeth and I. So talk," he said and took a short pause. "Please…"

"Fine. Did you sleep with her?" I asked him. The moment the question left my lips it felt like a huge weight had been lifted off my shoulders. I composed myself and sat across the room from him, not wanting to be seduced by his charming presence. If Johnny batted his eyes at me, I'd likely do anything he'd wanted.

There was a slight hesitation from him before he answered me. His words seemed as though they were a lie, but I wanted to believe him. "I didn't," He cut through the tension in the room. "I wanted to, I couldn't." He wanted to.

"You just… You were extremely comfortable kissing." *He wanted to. He wanted to.*

"We kissed… Frequently." *He wanted to sleep with her. He wanted to cheat on me.* Hearing the words felt worse than assuming and not knowing.

"Kissing is still cheating." *Don't cry, don't cry, don't cry.*

More hesitation. Was he thinking of more lies to tell me or contemplating telling full truths or just half-truths? I wanted to crawl into his brain and know everything. "Freddie, I... Need you... Like the air I breathe." His voice wasn't anything louder than a whisper. "I need you. I need you more than anything..." he paused again. "Please... Don't go. Don't leave me." *I'd like to deprive him of all that air he's breathing right now.* What he was saying to me was nothing but words, how was I supposed to know he meant what he was saying? I stared at him, his oceanic eyes were stormy. I could see the waves crashing against him, they could break me.

"Johnny... All your insecurities *never*... Made me blink once." I was bold and told myself to be brave, even if my thoughts were nothing but assumptions. It was all I had. Assuming the worst was all I could have done until now and I was right to, he was unfaithful to me. "I accepted it. I accepted you and I... I — I tried to be understanding but — But the... Unconditional love I felt for you before all of this... Suddenly feels a little more conditional than it used to be."

"I don't like who I am, Freddie." Maybe I broke him too, the same way he broke me. "I don't want to be the way that I am..." It sounded as though he was saying he didn't want this life. That hurt me. Would he rather live unhappily with some woman? With Elizabeth?

"Why is it okay for anyone else to be gay except you, Johnny?" I asked him. "Is it okay that — That I'm... gay? Is — Is that okay?" I grew nervous and couldn't help stammering words out, unsure if it was actually what I wanted to say.

"You're confident in who you are, you know what you want,

of course it's okay." *That doesn't make any sense.* He readjusted in his seat and looked down as though he knew that what he was saying was contradictory to what he believed.

"I question myself more times in a day than I'd care to admit, but I can't tell you that because... Well because what good would that do for you?" I diverted eye contact. "How could you look someone who hurt you in the eyes and tell them they hurt you?" I asked him. "If I told you every time I doubted myself or doubted you, I don't think you would have stayed as long as you have. I don't know why you've stuck around, I'm basically a ticking time bomb — it's only a matter of time before I—"

"Don't." He was quick to snap at me. "I didn't know I hurt you so badly, you don't talk to me!"

"How couldn't you have known that you were tearing me apart? If it wasn't your mother, it was you and you didn't care because I'm just your roommate. That makes it okay to cheat on me, right? That makes it okay to kiss other people. To kiss women." *Oh great, here come the tears.* I wiped my eyes and looked at him. "Do you even want me, Johnny? Removing myself from your equation seems like it may make your choice easier for you."

"What choice, Freddie? I married you." He stood up, I thought he'd kill me right then for raising my voice back at him. "I — I look at you and... And the whole world fades away, it all gets better... And..." He was confused and didn't know what to say, he wasn't trying to lie to me. Lies roll off a tongue far quicker than the truth does. "I don't want to know another kiss from anyone else's lips but yours,"

"And Elizabeth's," I mumbled and immediately regretted it. It was gradual to me, but it was now clear that I wasn't the constant issue. He was more insecure than I'd known. "I don't want to leave you," I said to him, that was true, I didn't want to leave him. I'd considered it before, but I wouldn't be any better alone than I was with him.

"I don't want you to leave me." He walked over and kneeled in front of my chair. "I want to be with you the day we can remarry each other in the library." *He remembered that?* I allowed myself to sail off into his oceanic eyes, where the storms were clearing. He grabbed my hand and kissed my knuckles, then rubbed his thumbs over where he'd kissed. "Doesn't that sound nice? And a ceremony at the Bethesda fountain, where I saw you sitting, reading your backup book so you didn't look silly if I didn't show up. With your cute blue bowtie." The problem with Johnny was that while he *was* charming, he pretended not to care about all the little things. He pretended not to remember the smaller details that made moments what they were... Perfect. I shouldn't have second guessed him for a moment. Instead, I should have asked him what he'd thought. I should have trusted that he was overflowing with small amounts of loving memories instead of assuming he really didn't care. He wasn't perfect, but he was Johnny. And Johnny was mine.

"It sounds nice," I murmured to him and pressed my forehead against his. "I'm so mad at you," I admitted quietly. If the only person I had to talk to, *except my therapist* who I paid to have someone to talk to, was the one who hurt me, perhaps I should learn to let him in.

"I know." He pulled away from me and stood up again. "How can I fix it, Freddie? How can I make it better?"

"You can start by wearing your wedding ring. I know I can't change you, only you can change you." I hated our I'll only hold your hand in the dark kind of romance. I didn't want him to shout my name from the rooftops but I didn't want to be hidden. "I know you're someone I would fight forever for, but I need you to meet me halfway, it shouldn't feel like... Like a job sometimes."

"I want to make you so happy it cures your doubt." Johnny saying that let me believe that our sun would rise after our darkness had seemed to last forever.

I couldn't help but smile at him. "When did you meet Harriet?" I asked him.

"It would have been so smooth if you hadn't met the woman downstairs." He laughed at me. "I invited her to dinner."

"So did I," I let out a soft sigh. "And I'll just pretend you thought of it yourself." My forgiveness was sealed with a kiss. I fought with myself to not think about where his lips had been the entire time. I pulled away and he pecked the tip of my nose before returning to the kitchen to finish washing the dishes. It felt a little less domestic with him now that I'd known the truth. Forgiving him meant forgetting what he'd done, not thinking about it any more was going to be difficult. The bruise was still fresh enough that I'd still tasted Elizabeth's cherry flavored lipstick on his lips, which I'd promptly wiped away once he wasn't looking. I didn't enjoy feeling as though her hooker lips had just touched mine. It felt wrong and made me uncomfortable. At least Johnny's ass looked cute while he walked away from me.

I'd never be able to start the next chapter of our life together if I continued to re-read our past ones. I was willing to work on forgiving Johnny completely. Perhaps living in a movie wouldn't be so bad, Johnny and I could sell the apartment and everything we owned, we could travel the world and go on the adventure of a lifetime together. I didn't have to live life as though I was diagnosed with a death sentence. I could quit my job too and go to work with Johnny. I could do things I'd never done before. We could adopt a dog and move upstate, anything was possible. The only issue that would stand in my way would be Johnny's job, he loved teaching children and I would never ask him to give that up. Perhaps we could move to Africa and build schools with the missionaries. He could teach underprivileged children to read and write. How amazing would that be?

I slept soundly wrapped in my husband's arms that night. It was the first night in a long while that I'd fallen asleep without a worry in the world. It was the first time in my life that I'd allowed myself to do so. We could lie here for years or just hours, as long as I was wrapped up with Johnny. I dreamt about traveling to less-fortunate countries with him, I dreamt about teaching little children English and staying in a small hut under the stars. I dreamt how limitless life could be if I'd only let loose, if I allowed myself to entirely forgive my husband's actions, his words. Sometime during the night I'd woken up to Johnny's fingers twirling my messy stray hairs. It worried me that in the midst of my good dreams, he was having nightmares. I may have made peace with my situation but perhaps he hadn't.

"You're troubled," I sleepily teased him, sitting up a bit to readjust myself in his arms.

"No, Harriet, go back to sleep." He smiled at me and pushed my hair back, his eyes grazed over my face and he kissed the scar on my forehead from all those years ago. "I promised to protect you when we married, how could I have known you'd need protection from me," he whispered to me. *Oh, my love.*

How was I supposed to answer him? I reached up to his face and brushed my fingertips over his bottom lip. "I forgive you." I meant that. I was anxious that I'd never be able to tell him that honestly, but once the words left my lips, I was cured of the doubt I'd felt about him. *Happiness cures doubt.*

Chapter 11

I put in my two weeks at work and quit my therapist the next morning. I would confide in Harriet from then on. If I knew anything, it was that no one deserved to be lonely, not even the elderly woman sitting on the bench outside our apartment building. Johnny and I adopted a dog from the shelter and named him Archie, he was a smaller breed, technically called a Cavalier King Charles Spaniel. The same King Charles I, picked fights with parliament until he was executed. I thought it was unjust to name such sweet creatures after those of poor character, so when people asked what breed he was I told them he was a Cocker Spaniel and then made a gay joke about cocks. He had short curly hair and floppy ears with brown spots. He was a sweetheart. He gave me something productive to do while Johnny worked. I'd pick up Harriet from the bench outside and we'd walk him throughout central park. Every Wednesday evening, Harriet would come upstairs and have dinner with Johnny and I. Everything was exceptionally perfect, the only thing I wouldn't let myself give into was adopting a child. The adoption applications that Johnny had brought home remained in the corner of the bar in our kitchen, collecting dust. I had allowed myself to be at peace with my predicament, however, I couldn't justify adopting a child only to leave them with one less parent than they'd started with. Children deserved happy and healthy family homes, especially after being put through the wringer most of their life. It might have been confusing and harmful to their mental health, if a new parent suddenly disappeared and the other parent they were left with, eventually started dating. It was harmful to my spirit just knowing I would linger around with Archie out by the bench, seeing my living husband with other men, I'd likely start haunting the apartment to scare them away.

The first snow of every winter is always the best one, it always made the entire city go quiet. No bustling cars or people, no one outside yelling other than when morning comes and children come out to play in the fresh white powder that covered nearly everything. It was nearing the holiday season again, the best time of year, my favorite time of year and I wasn't alone or sad. I had put together my own quirky family to care for. Johnny and I, our dog Archie and Harriet... Along with her ghost husband Archie. I didn't care if it was too soon, by the end of October I'd put up our Christmas lights and Johnny would take Archie to buy a small Charlie Brown tree for our apartment. The best part was watching Archie bounce around in the snow while he walked Johnny, he was so full of energy that we couldn't keep up most of the time. The vigor of the holiday season always made me inexplicably happy, the music alone made me want to share my heart with strangers. It's the time of year for kindness, who wouldn't want to share that? Johnny that's who.

I'd sat happily on our sofa watching the lights around our window twinkle when he walked through the door with the most welcoming of smiles. He walked over to me and handed me a single flower that smelled like heaven.

"I stole it off the flower cart down the block," He kissed me. *Oh, those squishy clouds.* He took his jacket off and unwrapped his scarf from around his neck, he looked at me while he hung them up onto the coat rack. "You look like you're enjoying yourself."

"Stealing a flower…? For me? Scandalous." I twirled the stem between my thumb and index finger, the different colored lights reflected onto the white petals and I smiled at him. "You're home late, was everything all right at work?" I asked him and Archie greeted him. He yapped and leaned against Johnny's legs to be pet.

"Parent-teacher conferences were tonight, I apologize, I thought I told you." He picked up Archie and sat him next to me on the sofa, he sat down as well. "Did you have any… Specific plans in mind for Thanksgiving?" he leaned against me while he gave Archie a few pats on the head.

"Well, no, I thought we'd invite Harriet over, maybe our neighbors too if they're not busy," I said to him and rested my head onto his shoulder. "Why? Did you have any specific plans for Thanksgiving?"

"You can say no," he sat up and readjusted himself so that he was facing me. "My family invited me and a guest to their party on Thanksgiving," He gently picked up my hand and brushed his thumb over my knuckles. "I was thinking that you, my… My husband… Would want to accompany me… To the party?" His soft composure and sweet glance made it hard to say no to him. What if it went badly? Would it ruin the holiday season for me? What would going to this party mean for me?

"When you say… Party…" The look on my face should have let him know how worried I was. "Your parents live in New Jersey." I knew that going would mean I had to stay the night, if Johnny's father didn't know about us, that meant I'd be separated from him. I didn't want to feel alone and unsafe in his parents' home. Let alone feel that way on one of my favorite holidays, or any holiday at all. What did his parents have to feel thankful for, anyway? They were both awful people, they were so lucky that

God hadn't smote them yet. "We'd be... Staying?"

"Just overnight," He assured me. "One night, we'll leave in the morning."

Perhaps it was the kind nature of the holiday season pushing me in the direction to say yes, or perhaps it was the fact that Johnny had been so lovely these past few months I'd jump to do anything that made him happy. Whatever the case may be, I heavily considered agreeing immediately. Harriet would want me to give his family a second... Or in their case, a third chance to prove their own goodwill. I doubted the chances of the stay being something pleasant, but maybe I could manifest that somehow. Johnny and I had come from two different worlds. His family was wealthy and they didn't let you forget that they were in control for one moment, my family was one of the lower class. They didn't care much about anything but their' own path and we didn't speak much. To give a little insight, Johnny's parents paid for him to attend Columbia University in full, they were disappointed when he changed his major from business to a teaching degree because it meant he wouldn't be the next Donald Trump. My parents applauded me when I was hired by a bank without any prior working experience on my resume. I went to the college of 'I saved up enough money and bought a set of encyclopedias to read', a name in progress. Though there was a difference of education between the two of us, we were still able to hold intellectual conversation as if we'd both graduated Harvard at the top of our classes.

"I'll go with you," I said to him. "But we're staying in the same room..." I paused, forgetting my manners. "Please." I wasn't about to ask if he'd wear his wedding ring around his family, I'd grown to understand some insecurities would never change. "I don't want to be alone in that big house."

"It fits my parents' big egos." I could tell he was teasing, though I still appreciated the comment. I'd promise him that I would be nice to Vivian despite how she'd treated me that last time I saw her. I decided I'd be the bigger person, especially since my comments towards her weight made her feel as though she was the bigger person. She'd installed an in-home gym and hired a personal trainer when she got home. She should have installed an office and hired a personal psychologist for her bi-polar issues but calling her bi-polar would be an insult to those who actually were.

"And you'll stay with me?" I asked him again.

The hesitation in his voice made me feel guilty for asking. "Sure." Sure. If you're going to agree, at least act pleased about it. I didn't comment on his banal response. Johnny had an arbitrary way of expressing how he'd felt. It was almost messy and unsure, as though he'd spoken just to respond without a thought of what he'd said.

Would I be ready to face Vivian again come months end? I forgave Johnny long ago and I'd known she would hold a book to my nose and force me to re-read the last chapter of our lives together. She'd make a mockery out of me in front of Johnny's whole family. I felt that seeing her or even being in the same room as her would send me right back to my square one conundrum. If I decided later I didn't want to go, I could only hope that Johnny wouldn't be upset with me. He could have taken Harriet as his plus one instead, she'd be a real crowd pleaser. How many family members could possibly be at this party anyway? Are there people who can truly stand being in the same room as that woman for longer than two seconds? Between her egregious jokes and foul-smelling perfume, I got a migraine simply thinking about it.

My thought trail was interrupted by Archie's barking. He circled by the door and I knew he wanted to go outside. I left Johnny's side and hooked his leash onto his collar. "Come on, Archie," I said and opened the door for him. I'd grown accustomed to using the stairs instead of the elevator, hoping in some small way that it would tire him out before we'd get to the sidewalk where he began walking me rather than me walking him.

Archie and I walked almost side by side down to Columbus Circle and onwards down Broadway. I loved watching his ears flop back and forth as he trotted along, one stride of my own legs was about four or five for his little legs. I smiled and looked from his paws, back up so I'd know where we were going. I hadn't been afraid to walk alone at night in the city for years, but something about that evening felt off. So much so that I pulled on Archie's leash and stopped walking completely. I pushed my hair off my forehead and turned around to return home, I felt uneasy the whole way. I got turned around too many times to count and was sure I was being followed. I picked Archie up and stepped into the elevator, forgetting one of the only things I'd remembered from a self-defense class I'd taken after being fag-bashed outside of the subway. If you think you're being followed, don't lead them to your home. The elevator doors wouldn't close fast enough. Archie whined, I assumed because he didn't like being held for long periods of time. Once we'd gotten to our floor, I brought him inside and locked the deadbolt. I stared at the door handle for a moment before setting Archie down and removing his leash.

I virtually jumped out of my own skin when Johnny approached me. "How was your walk?" He kissed my cheek and finished locking the door. He twisted the doorknob to make sure it was locked and slid the chain through the slot.

"It was fine. It was quick, Archie did his business," I said. "It's bedtime, no?" I moved away from him and went to our bedroom. I changed into my bed clothes and closed our curtains, then climbed under the covers. Johnny followed behind me and plopped Archie onto the bed.

"Is everything all right?" He asked me and I smiled and nodded.

"Just got spooked, you know I don't like the dark." I lied to him. I sank into bed and closed my eyes, going over what I'd seen on my way home. The people I'd passed, the trees, the food venders. I kept seeing a taller gentleman, I originally thought he was a police officer. He looked so familiar but I couldn't wrack my brain enough now to find where I'd remembered him from. I tried to push my anxieties aside for the night and nuzzled closer to Johnny once he joined me in bed.

Try as I had to push those anxieties away, I was up and down all night as well as several nights after that. I continued to have nightmares for weeks, it was times like these that I'd wished I hadn't left my therapist. Nevertheless, I persisted, sleepily. I got dressed for the day and helped Johnny pack the overnight bags for his parents' house. The only solace I had now was knowing how beautiful the drive to their house was. The yellow and red leaves on the taller trees made me think of the first day I'd met Johnny and the romantic comedies with Jennifer Lopez. I purposely missed the entrance to his parents' driveway at least three times so that I could continue to look at them while I drove. Their neighbors must have thought I was either insane or just another New Yorker who got lost in the mountains.

"Freddie, you'll have to make the turn eventually. You may as well rip off the band aid," Johnny said sympathetically. *Well, what did he know?*

"I know, I know, just… One more time," I mumbled and missed the turn once more. The exasperated sigh that came from Johnny directly after told me everything I'd needed to know. I needed to slow down and — after sitting at the brink of their driveway for a few moments — turn.

"Proud of you, baby." *I did not need the condescending tone, thank you.*

"Mhm, as you should be." I smiled. "Bye, honey, I'll see you tomorrow."

"Ooh, no, no. You promised." He thought he was sly and that I wouldn't see. He looked around to check for anyone who could see before he kissed my cheek. I let it slide and simply indulged him, leaning into it.

"Okay, okay." I shut off the car and exited the driver's side. Their home was undeniably beautiful. Something had to be, otherwise no one would come around once they'd gotten to know what their personalities were like. I picked our bags out of the trunk and followed my husband into hell. He was able to sneak the two of us upstairs to his old bedroom to settle in before the chaos. I appreciated the act of regard to my anxiety more than he'd known and more than I could express. I set our bags on his bed and looked around the bedroom. It was as if I was teleported to a completely other world, I thought I'd known who my husband was but I didn't know half of him. I walked around his room and looked at the photographs hanging on his wall, gently brushing my fingers over the frame. "They clean in here often," I said, surprised, I was sure my own parents had turned my bedroom into a craft room they'd never use. He had so many sports trophies on the shelves with ribbons hanging off the sides of them, displayed proudly, I could only assume. "You were part of the equestrian team?" I teased lightly. "Isn't that... a lady's sport?"

"The ladies loved me, what can I say?" He sat on his bed and watched me walk around his room. I'd glance at him every once and awhile and smile.

"You can't keep staring at my ass, Johnny, not in your parent's house." I turned back to his dresser and picked up a photograph of him as prom king, it made me laugh a little seeing him so involved.

"It feels so scandalous doing what's not allowed under my parents roof again," he said. "Besides, those jeans are doing wonders for your cheeks."

"Again?" I asked, almost absentmindedly. I'd always wondered what Johnny's childhood was like and why he'd kept it a secret, it never dawned on me that it was to keep me from feeling bad about my own childhood, which was all I could assume.

"I was quite rebellious," he explained. "If my parents didn't want me to do it, well... It's what I would be doing." I loved hearing him speak so openly about himself. It made me love him more, if that was even possible. I took the prom king crown off his shelf and placed it atop his head. He truly was prince charming, the crown still fit. He lifted himself and kissed me briefly before putting the crown back.

"I'd love to show you everything in this time capsule, but we should go downstairs for a little while at least," he said and I nodded in agreement. That was what we came for, after all. He offered me another soft kiss before leading me down stairs. I'd hardly call a family gathering a party, more along the lines of a reunion where everyone gets together and ridicules each other for how they live their lives. It sort of made me appreciate how little contact my parents had tried to initiate with me. However, seeing everyone smile and run to him with open arms made me feel better about coming. Aunts and uncles, cousins and spouses of loved ones all greeted him. The moment I'd dreaded came quicker than I'd imagined. Vivian reached out with her old, saggy arms and embraced Johnny.

"My boy! I haven't seen you in months, we missed you." I swear she left a big, ugly, red lipstick stain on his cheek purposely. She looked at me with pure disdain in her eyes, though she smiled at me anyway. "Frederick, I hadn't heard from you. I'd assumed the worst. How's the cancer?" *Assumed or hoped for?*

"Well, I hadn't seen her in months. I assumed she was doing fine." The only cancer I was worried about was her cancerous presence in my marriage.

The smile across her lips faded only halfway and she pulled Johnny away to force him to mingle. He turned and mouthed a quick 'sorry' to me before he was out of sight. I found my own way to the bar and poured myself a drink. I'd quickly made an escape to an empty room to sit alone and watch the leaves blow in the wind out the window. As I'd finally gotten comfortable, I watched Charlotte walk in. She smiled at me, her smile was far warmer than Vivian's. Hers seemed sincere and welcoming, just like Johnny. "Am I allowed in here?" I asked, thinking she'd ask me to leave. It didn't matter how nice I thought her smile was, she was still Vivian's daughter.

"You can sit where you'd like." She leaned against the window frame, blocking most of my view out of it.

"Johnny invited me, I apologize for intruding." I tried to be nice, I hadn't spoken to her much alone. Just the one time when she invited me to her son's baptism, before I was immediately uninvited by her mother. "How's your… son?" Small talk was definitely not my strongest trait.

"Listen, I don't mean to intrude on your quiet time. I know my family is overwhelming, I just wanted to apologize on behalf of my mother." *That was unexpected.* I always assumed she'd felt the same way and that's why she stayed quiet, she was more like her brother than I imagined she'd be. "I know you make Johnny happy. He talks about you to me privately, he worries. He loves you, despite my parents trying to separate you."

"Thank you," Was all I'd thought to say. "I love him too." *Of course, I love him too.*

She watched me, as though she was thinking of something to say. Johnny did that often. "Are you getting treatment?" she asked quietly and I shook my head. I didn't want treatment. "May I ask… Why?" And I hesitated at first. Would this just get relayed to Vivian?

"When you're in love with someone, you cross oceans and mountains for that person. It would be cruel of me to make Johnny watch me die that way. I wouldn't want to watch him wither away, sick from the poison running through his body. He won't admit it to me, but I know deep down he feels the same way." I watched her. My eyes glossed over with tears and it made it hard to see. I sipped my drink to distract myself. "I would do anything to ensure that in the end, the love of my life was happy and… Able to move on without me."

"Frederick, if you think for a moment that he'll move on… Please tell me you know he won't just forget about you." Charlotte was sweet. If only I'd known to remove her from Vivian's presence sooner and unleashed the true person from the one hiding behind her mother.

"I would need him to, Charlotte. I'd never be able to move

on myself… If I knew he wouldn't someday be okay again." I sipped my drink again and set it aside. Charlotte was quick to move and pick my drink up to place a coaster underneath it.

"I'm sorry, the — The wood is old and it would get a ring where the glass was left, my father would kill you if the cancer didn't first." *That was blunt.*

I laughed quietly, making light of it. "I understand, thank you," I said. "I owe you now, you saved my life." I teased her. She was so easy to talk to. It must have been because of how alike she was to my husband, they had to have gotten it from their father. Not that I'd ever had a conversation with him but Lord knows they didn't get that from Vivian.

"Well, I should get back before my mother sees me alone with you. Next thing I know she'll start saying we're seeing each other." She leaned over and kissed my cheek. "Find me if you need some comfort." She smiled and walked back out. It gave me comfort to know that she was different and that I had a possible chance of having a relationship with Johnny's father if he ever told him the truth.

I stayed in that room and hid for most of the evening. I finished my drink hours before and watched the sun go down behind the red leafed trees. Disassociating and being able to lose time was a talent of mine. It was something I'd been worried about when I was younger, but when I learned to use it to my advantage, times like these flew by. The longer I sat there alone, the harder it was to fight sleep. Alcohol had always made me inconveniently tired. I suppose I was better off tired than drunk and stupid. I glanced to the door when it creaked open and perked up a bit when I saw Johnny step into the room. "Are you having fun?" I asked him as though I didn't already know the answer. He still had that god awful shade of lipstick smeared on his cheek.

"I'm actually going to bed, everyone started doing tequila shots outside and shot-gunning beer cans," he said softly. "I'm not a big drinker."

"I know," I struggled to get off the sofa, it was squishy and basically ate my bottom. "Can I come?" I asked him.

"That's why I came to find you, I was going to ask if you were tired," *God, yes.* I nodded and fixed the sofa. He led me up the stairs, back to his bedroom and he locked the door. "My uncle bet my mother he could down a beer faster than her, they're all going to be drunk and unbearable soon."

"Mm, I see." I didn't care, I was tired and ready for a good night's sleep. I had successfully avoided the haughty wrath of Vivian Burke and I felt it best to seal the victory with an approximate six-to-eight-hour nap.

"You're so sleepy, Freddie, did you have a drink?" He asked me. He pulled me close into his arms and kissed my lips. I hummed and nodded. "Oh, shame. No chance of canoodling under my parent's roof then." *What a low blow.*

"Well, that's quite an unfair offer you put on the table when I'd likely fall asleep mid-orgasm. It wouldn't even be my own, I'd fall asleep and you'd have one." I pressed my face into his chest, almost dozing off just then. Johnny laughed at me.

"Okay, Freddie, Okay, strip down to your boxers and I'll tuck you into bed, baby." He teased me, he could have continued to all night and it would still have gone straight over my dense head.

The rest of the night was a complete blur. I woke up with a pounding headache and a missing husband. When I looked at the clock, I realized that I had overslept, it was almost eleven o'clock and everyone was probably already awake. I quickly grabbed my clothes and dressed myself. I brushed my teeth and combed my hair back before I went downstairs to deal with what I could only hope would be a hungover and irritated Vivian, she was simply making teasing her too easy.

As I walked into the kitchen, I was greeted with sleepy smiles and relatives still in their pajamas. "Happy Thanksgiving," I said softly. Johnny brought me a cup of coffee and I thanked him. I followed him back into the kitchen. "Good morning," I smiled at him, I fought the urge to lean in and kiss him. "Do you need help cooking breakfast? I don't mind," I said.

"Happy Thanksgiving," he responded. "Could you whisk the milk into the eggs?" He asked and I nodded. "It makes them fluffier." Vivian and Johnathon both made their way into the kitchen. I poured them both coffee and extended Johnathon's to him while letting Vivian pick up her own.

"I didn't see much of you last night, you didn't greet me," Johnathon said to me. "I expected a hello at least, my son was kind enough to allow you to come to our home for our family holiday." He sipped his coffee.

"I tell Johnny all the time to find a more respectful roommate, hubby. Still, he keeps him," Vivian responded to her husband. I received a sympathetic glance from Charlotte. I finished my cup of coffee and washed my cup.

"I didn't want to interrupt," I said quietly. It seemed waking up in a strange house wasn't enough, I would be interrogated to the third degree before breakfast. Even though I'd forgiven Johnny, it still stung when Vivian referred to me as his roommate.

"Look at me when you speak to me, it's incredibly rude to speak to someone with your back turned." I thought I was being polite by washing what I used. I turned and looked at him, I apologized and went to whisk the eggs as I was asked. "Johnny, have you spoken to your cousin Karen? She's looking for a roommate in the city. Your mother told her about your apartment, she's interested." There wouldn't be a relationship between this family and I ever. As they continued to speak as if I wasn't standing there it became clear to me that I didn't want one anyway. "Let me know when your friend Hedrick moves out, Johnny. Karen has agreed to pay half your rent." Johnny raising his voice had become a semi-regular occurrence as of late. First there was the hospital, then when we were fighting about him and Elizabeth and right now. That's three times within a year, when before, I'd never heard him yell in all the time I'd known him. His brows furrowed and he'd never looked sexier.

"Freddie isn't moving out!" He snapped at them. I was worried that I might suffer from the ramifications of what I felt he was about to say, no matter how much I wanted him to say it. There was a room full of shocked gasps, I could only assume that they were surprised Johnny had the balls to scream at his father, that or they too had never heard Johnny raise his voice. "His name is Frederick, not Maverick, not Hedrick, and he's not my roommate, he's my husband. I... I—" He stammered for a moment, coming off his high. "I married him." He deflated a bit, realizing what he'd admitted. I, however, was quietly overjoyed. Suddenly I'd had everything in my life. I watched his father and looked at the expressions amongst his family. Everything was quiet for an uncomfortable amount of time before anyone dared speak.

"I know," was all that Johnathon said. His tone was one of disappointment. If he had known the entire time, why didn't he say anything? He exited the room and Vivian glared at me.

"Are you happy now, Freddie? You've ruined so many lives." *Oh, bullshit.*

"He didn't ruin anyone's lives, Ma," Johnny said. "You can

finish cooking breakfast for everyone, I'm taking my husband and I'm going home. I really hope that you all have a fantastic holiday." Now my husband was the one with the condescending tone. "I hope you choke on the wishbone." He left the room quicker than I could have noticed through all the stares coming my way.

"Bye, Freddie." Charlotte smiled at me. If I hadn't known anything else, at least I knew that she was happy for Johnny and I. I moved past Vivian and went outside to the car. Johnny was waiting in the driver's seat for me.

"I love you, Freddie." He looked at me. "Call Harriet, we can cook turkey at our apartment and invite the neighbors over." *Oh, Johnny.* I stayed quiet for a few moments while he drove away. It was hard for me to wrap my mind around what had just happened, it wouldn't matter how happy I was that he stood up to his family if it made Johnny sad, I didn't want the gesture. I took the time to try to read his expression before I realized I had been quiet for too long.

"Thank you, Johnny," I murmured to him and sat back comfortably for the rest of the drive home.

The holiday traffic on the way home nearly took up our entire day. By the time we'd found a parking spot, we didn't have enough time to cook anything. I promised Johnny that this was all right, we could order in from the greasy old Chinese restaurant we'd used to. Harriet would love it. We got back into our apartment and Johnny immediately spread out onto the sofa. I laughed at him and closed the door. Archie greeted me and I pulled his leash off the coat rack. "Do you want to pick up the food or take Archie for a walk?" I gave him two options for good measure. "Answer quickly, Archie is waiting," He groaned at me and stretched.

"Do I have to?" He yawned and I smiled.

"Okay, okay, I'll take Archie, you'll rest for ten minutes and then go pick up the food." I met him by his throne and leaned over. "Kiss me, I love you," I said.

"Kiss me, I love you back," he repeated and lifted himself enough that his lips smooshed mine. I laughed again, against him.

"I'll be right back." I hooked Archie's collar and he pulled me right back out of the apartment. I walked our dog down the stairs and outside along Central Park. The sun was nearly set and the clouds were beautiful, shades of pinks and purples. It was my favorite color of twilight. I let Archie lead me where he wanted so I could watch until there was no light left in the sky.

I looked down at him and he looked up at me. "What are you looking at?" I asked him happily. My life was perfect. My eyes welled over with tears and for the first time in forever it was out of pure happiness. "Let's go home, Archie," I said. He wagged his tail and pranced alongside me. I missed my dog while we were away and I stopped to pet him before we went back upstairs. I glanced over to the park bench across the street to see if Harriet was there. "I guess she's home today." I kissed Archie's head and stood, I turned around only to run into who I thought was the same man I was afraid was following me weeks prior.

I simply smiled to mask the fact that I was terrified. "I'm so sorry. Have we met?" I asked to be polite. It was dark now and the yellow-lit street lamps did no favors for my vision. I suddenly felt I was being irrational, I had always been afraid of the dark. Of course, I imagined this too. "I didn't mean to bump into you. Have a good holiday," I said and walked into my apartment building. At least in there I could see who I was speaking to. I pressed the elevator button.

"Are you Frederick?" He came into my building. I looked at

him, trying to remember where, if at all, I had met him.

"I — Yes," I responded and pressed the button to summon the elevator again. "Do I know you?" I began to worry. I watched the countdown of the floors.

"You wouldn't remember me," he said. "We only met once, briefly. I've waited to run into you again," *What?*

Eighteen, seventeen, sixteen, fifteen. The elevator wasn't coming fast enough. I picked up Archie and went for the stairs. I looked at him. "I have to get back to my spouse… Happy Thanksgiving."

"You're husband." He was quick to correct me. *How did he know that?* He was a burly man. My eyes traced the outline of his figure and it immediately became clear how I knew him, where I knew him from. I let Archie fall from my arms. I stared at him, trying to get a glimpse of what his face looked like. "My son was given life in prison because of you, charged with attempted murder, but you deserved it. Faggot." I knew my world would be ending the moment I heard the gunshot. At first, I was unable to distinguish the ding of the arriving elevator from the ringing in my ears. I was so focused on trying to remember who he was, I hadn't noticed the gun in his hand. I had always been happily naive to what people were capable of, the same sort of density stuck even after the first time he and his son beat me for… being the way I was. Even through all my insecurities, I was always so proud of myself for being true to who I was, this was the only moment I found where I wasn't. *Where is Johnny?*

The bullet left his gun and entered my lower chest. It felt as though everything moved in slow motion. I didn't have many thoughts before everything turned into a pitch-black nothingness.

I woke up once with clouded vision and a soft wind against my face. There was distorted beeping and too many blue people

113

talking. My head throbbed and a light shined into both of my eyes. The blue people moved too fast around the room I was in and the beeping only seemed to get louder. My eyes fluttered closed for only a second before a dome was pressed to my face and I felt pain. I thought I was screaming but nothing came out. I was trapped inside myself. A blue person hovered over me and there was more muffling, something about... Having a bullet removed. Was someone hurt?

Chapter 12

Driving in the midst of all the holiday traffic was beyond tiring and I wasn't even behind the wheel. Before we'd crossed under the Holland Tunnel to get back into the city, Johnny thought it would be a good idea to get some fresh air. We parked along Hudson Street in Hoboken and went to sit at the Grundy Park pier to watch the sunset against the Manhattan skyline. It was completely empty, not a soul in sight. The lack of others made Johnny feel comfortable enough to offer affection as we'd sat on a bench at the end of the pier. I happily accepted all he had to give. I let out a breathless giggle when he nipped the softer skin on my neck and I propped my legs over his lap.

"Johnny," I smiled and leaned into him each time he'd touched me, I hadn't cared how touch starved it led him to believe I was. I adored him. "We should talk about what happened at your parent's house, no?" I whispered and met his lips halfway to mine. I could have kissed him there forever without ever needing anything else, but I had questions. I laughed against his lips. "Johnny, seriously,"

"All right, all right." He readjusted himself and laid his head against my chest. We both watched the boats that trotted along in the water.

"Are you all right?" I asked him and he nodded. I hesitated a moment, battling an internal war with myself. I didn't want him to pull away from me if I pushed him too much. "What are you thinking about?"

"Sex," he teased me. I whacked his thigh and chuckled.

"Sex with me, I hope." I kissed his cheek. It continued to amaze me the level of intimacy we'd continued to have after every obstacle that had been thrown into our laps. I couldn't bear the thought of a day where I'd have to love again. It sent chills down my spine thinking I'd ever have to give my heart away to anyone else. I would rather spend every day alone for the rest of my life than have to live without him. The chills could have also been a side effect of the breeze coming off the water. It was always colder by the water's edge. "Johnny, tell me how you really feel," I said softly. I hid my face in his hair in an attempt to hide my nose from the nippy air.

"Did you just smell me?" *Stop changing the subject.*

"It's hard not to, you smell wonderful." I lifted my face out of his curls. His hair always smelled so wonderful. "Now stop avoiding me," I ran my fingers through the back of his hair. His curls folded into perfect triangles that dispersed when they met the back of his neck.

"He knew Freddie, he pretended not to," he said finally. I could feel how much it bothered him. I was confused by the comment too. How could he have known and kept it quiet? Or been okay pretending not to know? It would have eaten me alive keeping such a big secret to myself. "I don't understand why," he said. I didn't understand either. I was trying to think of anything that could possibly have given Johnny some sort of insight.

"Maybe… He just didn't want to lose you?" I suggested. It was all I could think of on such short notice. Even if it were true, he wouldn't have lost Johnny. Just the way he perceived Johnny. A perfectly athletic and charming son, a gorgeous prom king, the equestrian team captain? That last one still baffled me. The ladies loved him, yeah? Well probably not as much as I did.

"He wanted to believe I was still someone he could relate to," Johnny repeated what I said, however, in a far more intellectual way. It made more sense than what I suggested to him. It made more sense than anything I could ever think of to tell him. "We used to be very close."

"I don't see why you can't be just as close." I traced invisible shapes along the back of his neck. "He's just being hard headed," I murmured to him. The sun was nearly set behind the tall buildings that made up most of the city. The clouds were the perfect balance of stringy and fluffy, a beautiful shade of pink and purple. They had always been my favorite color of twilight. I was distracted momentarily by the palette of colors. I looked down at Johnny. "We could go back," I said softly to him. "We don't have to cut them out... You... Don't have to cut them out."

"I do if it means making you miserable," he explained. "What would I do without you, Freddie? If I keep them... who will be there to grow old with me? Who will love me when I'm no longer just a pretty face? When I have wrinkles and a saggy ass?" I fought laughter and couldn't hold back the smile.

"Well... me, Johnny." I picked up his face and kissed his lips. "I will." I hadn't known Johnny worried about the same domestic things I did. About who would be there, what we'd look like. Me, I would be there. I would always be there. This was the first moment that I'd realized that Johnny would be there too. That Johnny planned on growing old with me too. Happiness flowed through my veins, this was just the perfect amount of serotonin I'd needed to get through the rest of my days. I held his face firmly and kissed him again. "You're going to be a sexy old man. God will smite anyone who disagrees."

"Oh, will he? He'll smite anyone who thinks I'm not?" He smiled against my lips. Oh, he smiled. God would smite anyone who thought he wasn't beautiful inside and out, I would make sure it happened. As long as they didn't act on their feelings, we could walk down the street together and people could tell him he was pretty all day long. I would just agree with them.

"If not God, I would do that for you," I whispered back to him. "You deserve to be told just how incredibly beautiful you are."

"Freddie, you are an alluring man," he said. "Don't butter me up now and not put out later."

"Mhm, you wish I'd butter your buns later." I giggled and sat up. "You're missing the sunset," I said to him, there are moments in everyone's life when everything goes quiet. A moment so gratifying that it replaces all the bad moments. A moment when you know you're in the right place, a place where you know you will be safe forever. I felt as though this was mine. Quiet, by the water, watching the sunset. There was nothing that could possibly ruin this day, not even Vivian herself.

When I allowed myself, I relaxed against the piers bench. The curved back fit perfectly against my own. I closed my eyes and let the cool breeze doze me off into a light sleep. I could still hear the water splashing against the piles of the nearby docks and the birds chirping as they flew into nearby trees. In the midst of the darkness that flooded my closed eyes, I suddenly no longer felt the weight of Johnny on my chest. I opened my eyes and was met with more darkness. There was a single flickering light at the other end of the pier. I got off the bench and made a run for it, immediately feeling it would be safer to sit under it. The light bulb cracked and sparked in front of me when I reached it, the loud noise of electricity startled me and then everything was dark again. My ears were ringing, it was uncomfortably loud and made my head throb. I was turned around by the sound of my husband's voice and I shouted his name, I couldn't see him, I'd barely heard him. *Please speak up, it's all muffled.* My thoughts were raucous.

I was turned around again by music and laughter. I began to cry when I saw Johnny, but it wasn't him. It was an image of his chest, and my face was buried in it. I was overwhelmed with a wafting scent of his shampoo, then his cologne. He was humming our wedding song as we danced and then it all went away again. I'd fallen to my knees and screamed for anyone to help. The ground felt soft, wet and cold. I shivered in fear that I'd never find another face and I grabbed my chest. Pain, I let myself go and searched around for light, it was farther away this time. I got to my feet and ran to get to it again. Each step I took it felt as though the new flickering lamp got farther away from me. I looked at my hands when I could see them in the distant lighting, it immediately halted my pace. They were red. Blood? Then there was more pain. When I looked up, the light had stopped flickering and was now only a few steps away. It felt instinctive to step into it, I was telling myself that I'd be safer there. Another part of me wouldn't allow my feet to move from where they'd been planted. That other part felt afraid of the light, it told me that everything would end. The hurt I was feeling was incredibly heavy. For a moment, everything was quiet and the birds started chirping again. I heard Johnny's voice. He was sad, what did I do? Why was Johnny crying? Panic flooded through my entire being and I turned away from the light to listen to what he had to say.

"Freddie," His voice was so quiet, I walked further away from the lamp so I could hear him. "If you wake up… We — we can go home, doesn't that sound nice?" *Where are we, Johnny?* His voice sounded broken, I ran towards it. "I can't be strong without you, Freddie, don't you see? I'm selfish, you can't leave me."

The panic grew tighter in my chest. *Leave Johnny? No, no, no, no, no! I'm here! I'm — I'm not ready to die, not yet. Not yet. Not yet.* I collapsed back to my knees and looked around for help again, the light behind me showed me that I hadn't gone far. *Johnny, hold me, hold onto me. Not yet.* It felt empty inside without the image of him behind his voice. I lay on the ground, on my back, and breathed. It was my only attempt to calm myself down. I closed my eyes. Where was I? What did I hear? I heard Johnny. He was crying, begging, praying. Johnny never prayed. I heard machines humming. Machines beeping. A squeaky door. What could I see? Light. Red light through my eyelids. And if I opened them? Johnny. I could see Johnny. I could see a hospital room. *I was in a hospital room.* There was a mask on my face and I was in a hospital room.

I glanced around the room and thought I could get up. I was mistaken. *Why can't I move?* Everything hurt, my head was throbbing. None of which mattered at all, Johnny was there. I watched him, internally begging him to look at me. Could he see me too? *I need help, Johnny, what's happening? Look at me. Look at me.* The machines in the room began beeping louder, I groaned at the noise. I knew Johnny could hear it because it was the first time in what felt like forever that I was able to hear myself, no matter how muffled it was. The next thing I knew, the squeaky door opened. Twice. A nurse and a doctor. A flashlight shined into each of my eyes and my pulse was checked, then a needle was pushed into my arm.

"What are you giving him?" Johnny asked the nurse. He sounded exhausted and desperate. *What happened?*

"A mix of morphine and saline." She'd answered him quickly and pulled down the mask that covered my face. I had trouble breathing without it and gasped, she immediately replaced it with a new one.

Everything happened quickly. They were making sure I was okay. *Make sure Johnny is okay too.*

"Can he speak?" Johnny asked them as they left. The nurse gave him a little nod.

"Not at first probably, but he can hear you. You can talk to him." And she left. I received a sympathetic look from my husband. The one I gave him was something more confused. *What's going on, Johnny?*

"Someone hurt you, Freddie. Do you know who?" *No, baby, please don't cry.* Not that he could hear me. I was trapped inside myself. It felt suffocating. I could move my fingers. I could move my face, my head. I shook my head at him a little. I didn't know what was happening. "Do you know what happened?" He asked me, and I shook my head again. He simply nodded. He stood up and leaned over towards me. His soft clouds pressed against my forehead. *I could feel that.* I closed my eyes. I couldn't help but let tears fall, I felt so helpless. The only thing that brought me peace was that I could see him. He was standing in front of me, he was talking to me. He grabbed my hand and squeezed it. I found comfort in feeling his palm against my fingers. It made me comfortable enough to close my eyes again. I just listened. I listened to Johnny. I listened to myself.

When I got up again, I was back home in our apartment. Archie was curled up in his bed by the Christmas tree. It's A Wonderful Life was playing in the background on the television. Johnny was standing in the kitchen doing the dishes, wearing our apron with the peaches on it. "Can you hear me?" I asked him. He turned around and looked at me, he smiled. Oh, he smiled. I ran to him and crashed into his arms. "Don't let me go," I whispered to him, I held him as tight as I could.

"Freddie, baby, what's going on? What's wrong?" He asked me, he rubbed his palms up and down my back, massaging me. "Are you all right?" His voice was soft and sincere. He pulled himself away from me so that he could see my face. "Freddie?"

I shook my head quickly. "I had a bad dream, it's over now. Can I help you with dinner?" I asked him. He kissed the tip of my nose.

"The turkey is in the oven, so is the stuffing. I cut the cranberry sauce, and the yams are in the toaster oven keeping warm. Waiting for the marshmallows." He hummed. "Switch on the radio," I looked at him and let him go. I turned our DVD player on and switched it to the radio setting. I turned on softer Christmas music.

"I love this song." I turned the volume up a bit. 'O Holy Night' made me want to cry whenever I heard it. It was exceptionally divine, it never mattered who sang it. It was soft and powerful all at the same time. Johnny took the opportunity to pull me close to him again.

"Are you leading or following?" he asked me.

"Well, you're the one with the apron on." I teased him. I kissed his lips and rested a hand on his hip. The smell of Thanksgiving dinner wafted throughout the apartment, paired with the music. Being swept away on our non-existent dance floor was nothing less than perfect.

My husband was never anything less than perfect. I laid my head on his shoulder and quietly, slowly led him over the carpet. I didn't know how to dance, but prom king Johnny Burke did. Prom king Johnny Burke knew how to do most things well. Sometimes it was hard to believe that Johnny kept me. He brought me into his arms and made me Frederick Burke. We were

Frederick and Johnny Burke, Johnny and Frederick Burke.

I gently spun my husband and pulled him close to me again. I inhaled a deep breath for the sole purpose of smelling him for comfort. He smelled different. "Did you get new cologne?" I asked him quietly. He almost smelled the same, but something about it was new.

"No, Freddie," he responded to me. He nuzzled his face into the crook of my neck and kissed me. It tickled and I smiled at him. We stayed close to each other and continued to move together. The longer we stayed so close the more everything began to feel distorted. I picked up my head and looked around the room. It felt as though everything was misplaced. It was all slightly moved. I let him go and rubbed my eyes. When I looked again, everything in the apartment was crooked. I looked at Johnny with mild panic.

"What's happened to our apartment?" I asked him. "What's going on? Where are we?"

He gave me an empathetic look. He grabbed my upper arms and gently shook me. "Freddie, wake up," he said.

"What?" I stared at him. His face was twisted. He began to distort just as the room had.

"Wake up!" He yelled at me. Johnny never yelled at me. I opened my eyes and looked around the hospital room. Johnny stood there next to me, nearly hovering over me. His hands were on my upper arms and he made eye contact with me.

"I need you to try and stay awake, Freddie. Please, try to stay awake," he said to me. He let my arms go and brushed hair out of my face. "Stay with me, don't leave." His voice lowered into a whisper. I watched his eyes and grew incredibly confused. My body was tense and I tried to relax against the bed. Johnny let me go and crossed the room. He opened the door, I hadn't even heard anyone knocking.

"Dad." I listened while Johnny spoke. Why was Johnathon here? *Oh, I know, Vivian must have sensed I was in the hospital and sent her husband to finish me off.* "What are you doing here?"

"I called your apartment to speak to you. Some older woman… Harriet Dorsey answered. Told me what happened." They exchanged hard stares, not even a knife could have cut through the tension in the room. It was weighted enough to make me feel as though the air got heavier on my chest. *Go on, Johnathon, what happened.*

"She's a friend, she's taking care of our dog." Johnny moved so that his father could enter the room. He closed the door behind him and looked at me in a way that made me feel as though everything would be okay, even if I knew he was still worried. I only wish someone would tell me what it was about.

"You have a dog?" His father asked him. Johnny wasn't a big fan of small talk. His brows furrowed a bit and he sat down in the chair that he pulled over next to me.

"Why are you here, Dad?" he asked him. He sounded frustrated. I tried to reach for him so he could grab onto my hand. I guess I couldn't reach as far as I'd thought, I was only able to flip my hand over and reach for him with my fingers. Johnny must have still gotten the gist of what I was trying to do, he laid his hand on top of mine. "It's okay, Freddie." He looked at me. *No, baby, I'm trying to comfort you.*

"I thought you'd need somebody." He sat across the room from Johnny and I. "I thought I could… Support you… In your time of need." Johnny's hand squeezed mine, the other hand reached up and covered his face so that his father wouldn't see him cry. I felt the anxiety start to build inside my chest. It was tight and painful. I closed my eyes briefly. What I thought was only for a moment.

When I opened them again, Johnny was across the room with his father and a doctor. Had I dozed off? The doctor was hanging two x-rays onto the cork board on the wall. Were those mine? He used a red expo marker and circled three parts of each photograph.

"The bullet entered Mr. Burke's chest here," *A bullet?* The doctor pointed to where he'd drawn a red circle. "And exited here." He moved his hand to show them.

"What's the third portion here?" Johnny's father asked.

"A fragment of the bullet is still inside him, I've arranged to have it removed immediately," *I was shot? I was — I was shot?*

"Why wasn't it removed immediately?" Johnny snapped at him. I flinched.

"We couldn't have known it was there without an x-ray," The doctor remained level-headed. He obviously delt with angry and emotional people on a daily basis.

"What happens if it doesn't get removed?" Johnathon asked all the questions that Johnny should have been asking.

"It's a loose piece of metal inside him. Very close to his heart, if he moves the wrong way, it could puncture a vital organ," he explained. *I can't lose Johnny.* Johnny was a wreck. He started crying again, I didn't know if he'd ever stop.

"Get it out. Get it out." His hands trembled and he grabbed onto the end of the bed I was lying in. He looked up to me and managed somewhat of a smile. "Freddie, sweetheart, can you hear me?" I nodded for him. He crossed my bed side and sat on the edge. "You... I—" He audibly swallowed and wiped his cheeks. "Please don't leave me, I still need you," My own breathing stuttered and my eyes flooded, *I don't want to.* "I still want you," he whispered. "I know you're tired, but I don't want you to sleep forever." *I'm right here.*

"Rest isn't terrible for him now," the doctor said. "If anything is irregular, his heart monitor will go off."

"Thank you," Johnathon said and led the doctor out. He must have known that it wasn't helping Johnny to have him around. I wish I had gotten to know who his father truly was. God, I tried to. I tried to get to know his family.

My arms were sore and it hurt to move, nevertheless I persisted to try and lift them. Just one. I tried to pull the mask that covered my face away. Johnny gently grabbed my hands to stop me.

"No, no, please don't. Don't do that, it's helping you," he said and I shook my head, I couldn't speak with it on. I watched him helplessly. I waited for him to let my hands go before I tried to remove it again. He stopped me. "All right, just for a moment," he said softly. He was gentle, he pulled the mask down. He untangled the elastic from my ears and softly wiped the moisture off my cheeks.

I exhaled a deep breath that I'd held in. I looked at him, allowing the entire world to fade behind him. I watched his sad, stormy eyes. "Johnny…" My throat was sore and my voice was hoarse, I felt as though I hadn't had water in ages. Johnny cried and kissed my cheek. "I'm so… sorry…"

"No, no. It's not your fault. You have nothing to apologize for. Please, baby," he kept his face close to mine. I wished the world would end now. I didn't know what would happen to me, I didn't know if I would make it out of this. I didn't know if Johnny would make it out of this, but if the world would only end… At least I'd know that we wouldn't part ways. Instead, we lay there, together, cheek-to-cheek in our own personal hell of not knowing.

It was harder to breathe without the mask on, I had to fight for deeper breaths. "Don't... Remember me this way, Johnny," I whispered into his ear. His face was pressed into the side of my neck. His tears began to make the smallest puddle in the crease of my clavicle.

"I'll remember everything—" Johnny sobbed. He knew I was struggling. He carefully put the mask back onto my face. He used his thumbs to wipe away the residual tears under my eyes. Keeping my eyes open was hard. I felt exhausted. I knew that Johnny was too. I didn't know how long I had been there, I didn't know when the last time Johnny had slept was.

"Remember us how we... We used to be," I couldn't hear myself. I knew the mask muffled my voice. I didn't know if Johnny heard me either. I deflated against the bed and tried to relax. I allowed myself to close my eyes and sleep. I could only hope that Johnny would allow himself to sleep too. I could only hope that when I would wake up, this would all be a nightmare.

I awoke on my back and in the darkness again. This time it felt different, I wasn't scared to be there. I looked at my hands, they weren't red. There was no pain. I got back to my feet and walked over to sit by the light, they must have fixed the bulb in it, it no longer flickered. I sat on the soft ground next to it, it still felt safe. I looked backwards to where I'd come from. It was fuzzy, particles of small light danced together in the darkness. It felt chaotic. In the midst of it, it was no longer quiet, machines beeped and there was the low hum of fluorescent lighting and... Johnny's voice. I felt no attachment stepping back, but I did. I got up and stepped closer. I needed to hear Johnny. I needed to smell him. I needed to see him. I only wished he'd come near the light instead of hiding in the darkness.

I fidgeted with my wedding ring while I listened to him speak to me. The beeping of the machine I was hearing, with him, was becoming less frequent and everything started to become hazy. I still fought to listen. "Freddie," it was as if his lips were next to my ear. "I know you're tired. I know you're hurting." It was quiet for some time, there was nothing except the beeping.

"Johnny? Can you come out? I want to see you." I smiled and turned around to try and find him. "I'm okay."

"I'd — I'd like you to stay, Freddie," His voice was somehow quieter than before. "But I understand, if — If you need to... To—"

"Johnny, please don't cry, where are you?" I started to cry too. "Please come to me—"

"It's okay, Freddie," There was a gasp for air, and sobbing that echoed throughout the blackness. "You can — You can go," *I don't want to. Where are you?* "But please don't."

Before I could beg for his presence, the darkness went away and there was nothing but... light. I turned around to face it, *where had it come from?* I stepped closer to it. It was so warm. It was so inviting. All of the loud, worrying noises faded away and I felt sincerely safe. The light called to me and patiently waited for me. I looked back again to see if I could still find Johnny, but the voice that greeted me wasn't his or anyone's I'd ever heard before. "It's all right, Freddie. You don't have to go back."

"I'll lose Johnny." I stared into the light and suddenly even that felt okay.

"You'll only rest until Johnny can join you. You will see him again." I gave into it. I gave into the quiet, into the peace. I gave into knowing that it wouldn't be over. I gave into knowing I would see Johnny sometime soon.

I would never get my wedding on fifth avenue with Johnny.

We wouldn't move upstate together, nor would he inevitably talk me into adopting children with him, even under the circumstances. I wouldn't get the luxury of spending hours sitting upside down on our sofa, looking through old magazines and happily arguing about the style of sconces we'd put up after the house we'd just bought was renovated. I wouldn't see marriage equality in all fifty states. Most importantly, I wouldn't grow old with the man who saved me. With the man I needed more than I needed myself.

I saw everything and I made peace with it. I watched every moment of my life as though it was on replay. It felt as though I lived in black and white, until one day I found sunshine, after the longest and darkest night. I swore to love Johnny all of my life and I was true to it; from the moment I first saw him smile to our very first fight and every day after. Johnny saved me in more ways than one, I only wished I hadn't let him down so soon. I wished I could have given him more of myself instead of unintentionally leaving him in silence. I found solace in knowing that his father came through for him at the end, that he wouldn't be completely alone, he had Harriet and Archie. I'd watch over him and pray that he'd live his life to the fullest extent. I'd wait expectantly to see him again, to rest beside my husband. I closed my eyes to dream… Just one more time before it all ended completely.

I was sitting on a porch swing watching waves crash onto the sand. There were seagulls flying overhead looking for food. There was a cool breeze coming off the water that pushed a tangy smell towards our house as well as the scent from the mosquito repellant candle I'd lit. I'd grown to have wrinkles and a saggy ass and so had Johnny. He walked outside onto the porch with two mugs of tea.

"Lemon-lavender tea for my Sweet Pea," Johnny said. He moved slower than he used to. He was still sexy as hell. He sat down on the porch swing next to me and carefully handed me a mug.

"With honey?" I asked him, leaning close.

"Well… No, we're out, I used sugar cubes." He smiled. Oh, he smiled.

"Mhm. I forgive you." I chuckled and sipped my tea. It was so good. I reached over to him and intertwined our fingers together. "Has Harry called today?" I asked him.

"No, she has better things to do than to sit with her old dads." He looked at me and laughed. "She said she'd be here next weekend after spring break."

"She's so smart. Our daughter is going to be the next Michelle Obama." I set the mug down on our end table. "Our own Harriet Burke, bless her heart." Johnny squeezed my hand.

"I miss having her around," he admitted quietly. "It feels emptier."

"It feels like I haven't had time to fool around with my husband for twenty years and now I'm scared to let him see me nude." I laughed at him. "She visits us all the time."

"You're scared? I used to be so sexy." He sipped his own mug of tea. "Now my blood pressure is so high it makes my cheeks pink. Both sets." I watched him look at our hands. He brushed his thumb over the back of mine, tracing the short wrinkles and age spots that had developed over the years. I couldn't help but smile and appreciate the time I was allowed to have with him.

"You're still sexy," I murmured and squeezed his hand back. "You aged well." I however, had not. Johnny looked great, his salt and pepper hair was indescribably attractive.

"You're just saying that because we're married and you have an obligation to tell me I'm pretty." Johnny huffed into his mug and pushed the swing back a little.

"Johnny, my love, I have never been obligated to tell you how beautiful you are," I said softly to him. I picked up his hand and kissed his knuckles. "I would straddle you right now if I wouldn't end up breaking a hip or something in the process." I leaned against him instead and he laughed at me again.

"Oh, you would not, you act like you're ninety." He pushed my hair back and kissed my forehead. "You're uncharacteristically dramatic today," he teased me.

"Way to use big words to confuse my ninety-year-old brain." I teased him back. *Such a charming man.*

"Oh, hush." He gently grabbed my chin so that I would look at him. "You're wonderful and you know it." *No, I don't, tell me.* He brushed his thumb over my lips and looked between them and my eyes. "If you don't then I haven't done a good enough job of reminding you over the years."

"You've been just as wonderful," I murmured, staring at his lips. *Kiss me, you romantic fool.*

"Not always, but you put up with me." His voice was just as calming to me as the sound of the nearby ocean flowing onto the sand. It was soft and floated through the air, straight into my ears, causing me to melt as it always had.

"I tolerated you at best," I whispered back and met him halfway. His lips would always be the softest clouds. Whenever I fell down, I'd always been caught by them. He would always kiss me and make it better, as he'd done with everything. He was never someone I didn't want around, even when I was mad, even if I said I didn't.

This would be the part of my romance comedy movie where

the camera would pan outwards and the end credits would begin to roll onto the screen. All the while the remaining bits of the last scene played out as though it wasn't happening at all. As though it wasn't the end. I would like to believe that this wasn't where my movie ended. I would have hoped there was a sequel, then another and another.

He pulled his lips away from me and I leaned closer to meet them again. "Yeah, you only tolerate me." He brushed his lips over my cheek and left a soft peck before pulling away again. "You love me more than you'd care to admit to me, Frederick *Burke*," he said to me. *If only he knew.*

"I fear sometimes that if you knew how much I truly did, it would scare you away," I said quietly to him.

"Twenty years of marriage and I still scare you." He watched my eyes. "I love you too, Freddie," he murmured. "You've changed me." If he kept sweet-talking me, I'd happily break a hip for him. I felt as though I'd never stopped staring at him, since the day I met him. His intelligent eyes, his swoopy-doo hair, his smile. "You'll miss the sunset if you keep staring at me like that." I didn't care. Johnny was the only thing I didn't want to miss if I looked away for too long.

I looked out anyway. Johnny once told me that the sunset was nothing but proof that the end of something can always be beautiful too. "So when we part ways one day in death, or someone takes a last breath, if you loved them deeply enough; a beautiful love, it will never end with something as simple as death," he said to me, I hope that one day, when Johnny and I pass together in our sleep, that we turn into sunsets. So the whole world can look at our lives together and see how much I loved him.

CPSIA information can be obtained
at www.ICGtesting.com
Printed in the USA
BVHW091830021222
653303BV00007B/737

9 781800 747449